Adriana

By Rosemary Laurey

A lifelong vow of revenge, magic and a love that transcends both.

Adriana has dedicated herself to the destruction of the invading Astrians who murdered her family and destroyed her village. But when she meets an honorable Astrian, she is torn between her lust for revenge and the unexpected love for her avowed enemy.

Warning, this title contains explicit sex.

Nova

By J.C. Wilder

In the sequel to *Heart of a Raven (Paradox I)*, Nova is on the verge of seeing her life's ambition come true when she wins a Merman in a card game. Now she's on the run with her unwanted companion, and with her future in the balance, she finds that the pursuit of her goals could cost this man his life.

Warning, this title contains explicit sex.

Deep Waters

A Samhain Publishing, Ltd. publication.

Samhain Publishing, Ltd.
577 Mulberry Street, Suite 1520
Macon, GA 31201
www.samhainpublishing.com

Deep Waters
Print ISBN: 978-1-59998-299-1
Adriana Copyright © 2008 by Rosemary Laurey
Nova Copyright © 2008 by J.C. Wilder

Editing by Jessica Bimberg
Cover by Christine Clavel

Titled Paradox II, 1-59998-224-2
First Samhain Publishing, Ltd. electronic publication: September 2006
First Samhain Publishing, Ltd. print publication: July 2008

Contents

Adriana

Rosemary Laurey

Dedication

For Judy Norsworthy.

Chapter One

Distant hoof beats vibrated the earth under Adriana's feet. Hesitating only a few heartbeats, she clambered up the escarpment above the shrine and looked toward the distance, shielding her eyes from the low afternoon sun. A lone horseman cantered along the riverbank. Adriana watched until certain he wore the garb of an Astrian. Strange, he was not dressed as a soldier. No matter, an Astrian was an Astrian. Any would serve her purpose. This one looked very different, and he was alone. Recently, they had started traveling in bands too large to ensnare. Two and three invaders she welcomed. They were easy to separate in the mist, to wander lost in the woods, while she ensnared her chosen victim. A single Astrian was easy prey, and a fine offering to Rache.

Adriana had consecrated herself to Rache, the Goddess of Revenge, twelve years earlier. As a child of ten, she'd witnessed, with young and innocent eyes, the coming of the Astrians. She'd been gathering kindling in the forest when she had heard the thunder of warhorses and started to run for home but, tripping, broke her ankle. She'd dragged herself forward, calling for help, but had frozen into silence at the first shouts and screams. Huddled behind a growth of wild sweetberry bushes, she'd watched the distant smoke rise from what had been her village. The cries had continued long after nightfall, and by dawn, there had been silence. But by then, Adriana had known there was no one left to come to her aid.

$$\text{\large C\!R \;\; S\!O}$$

She sobbed herself asleep in the gray of the morning. Hunger woke her by mid-afternoon. Dragging her painful leg behind her, she stripped the bushes of all the berries she could reach.

It was high summer, the bushes and brambles heavy with ripe or ripening fruit, but even if she could live on berries and crawl to the brook for water, how could she survive? Unable to walk, she'd be a ready victim for the first hungry bear or wolf.

Maybe now was the time to drag herself home and hope for help, but she knew in her heart that the silence meant there was no one left alive. In utter despair and pain, she lay on the soft leaf mold and cried until her face was streaked with mud and bitter sobs racked her body. She was only partly conscious when someone touched her shoulder, but was instantly alert, her hands ready to claw and scratch.

"Don't be afraid," a soft voice said. "We will not harm you."

Adriana blinked and stared. Two tall women bent over her. They were dressed in light brown robes and hooded cloaks of mottled green and brown.

"Who are you?" She knew as soon as she spoke. They were wood witches, the creatures no one saw, but to whom her village left offerings of food and young animals at the sacred shrines. Were they going to take her?

She sat up and tried to scoot backward.

"Wait, child!"

There was kindness in the voice, but also command. Adriana was too tired to resist. Even with two good legs, she couldn't outrun these wood witches—crippled, she was helpless. But not hopeless.

"What would you do with me, women of the woods?" she asked, raising her fingers in the sign of protection.

The woman nearest smiled, tossing back her hood to reveal dark brown hair that framed her pale face. "We would like to help you," she said. "What is your name, child?"

"Adriana," she replied, flinching as the witch's cool fingers stroked her swollen ankle.

"They did this to you?"

"I tripped when I was running."

"Away from them?"

"I was collecting kindling for my mother. When I heard the soldiers coming I ran home, but I fell."

"That fall saved your life, Adriana. I am Eadwyn, and this is my sister, Eadyyl. She is a healer and will set your ankle."

They carried Adriana deeper into the woods and gave her an infusion of andine bark. As the potion took effect, Eadyyl set her ankle, wrapping it with poultices and splinting it with branches and strapping from her pack.

"Rest, Adriana," she said. "We will take you to our sanctuary. In two cycles of the moon, your leg will be strong enough to walk on."

Two moon cycles was too long! "I want to go home!" Not deep into the woods with witches.

"It is not possible," Eadwyn said gently. "You cannot go home."

"But I want to!" Adriana shrieked in her anguish. "I want my mother! I want to see my brothers and sisters and my loft over the mill. I want to play with the puppies!" She broke into wild sobs, beating her head on the ground and wailing aloud her fear and misery.

Eadwyn held her close, rocking and soothing with gentle lullabies until Adriana had cried it all out. She stayed on Eadwyn's lap, leaning against her breast as she had as a small child on her mother's knee. "I want to go home," she sobbed, without the slightest hope that she would ever leave the woods.

"If you wish, we will take you home," Eadwyn said, "but, Adriana, there is no one there."

They carried her back through the woodland paths. From the rim of the trees, she saw smoke rising like gray plumes from the still-smoldering thatches. As they crossed the fields, no dogs barked and not a single cow lowed from the milch meadow. The gates to the pig sties hung open, the porkers being fattened for wintertide lying in pools of their own blood.

Adriana shuddered, but worse was to follow. In the village square, where they'd danced a few weeks back for May morning, grisly dancers hung from the maypole, their bodies slashed and mutilated. In the center of the square, where the high table had been set for her cousin Jaynew's wedding, there was a stack of bodies—men, children, dogs, goats and women all heaped together. As they crossed to the mill, she did not want to look, but horror compelled her. By the stable door, one of the puppies lay on the flagstones, his head crushed. Inside she found her brother, Bryn, his throat cut and flies covering his face and neck.

"Why?" she asked. Who could do this to others?

"They are Astrians," Eadwyn replied.

Adriana found her mother and father in the kitchen, their mutilated bodies thrown against the wall. Her two sisters and Cam, her baby brother, were speared to the walls of the pantry.

"Is there no one left alive?" Adriana asked.

They searched the village. Everybody who'd made up Adriana's life had been slaughtered. The stench of bodies ripening in the afternoon warmth filled air that had once smelled of baking bread, or the boiling of jam or the dipping of winter rushes in beeswax.

The life she'd known was utterly destroyed.

Adriana's eyes smarted with tears as she looked up at Eadwyn and Eadyyl. "Why would anyone do this?"

"They are Astrians."

"I hate Astrians." She spoke with the vehemence of a child who has nothing, not even hope.

"Come with us, Adriana," said Eadyyl. "We will heal your ankle and teach you our ways."

CR ∞

They had taught her well, and she'd been an eager pupil, learning to weave mists and shape spells. The Astrians forced the vanquished peasants to abandon the old groves and shrines in favor of stone-walled houses for their conquering Gods and priests. With Eadwyn and Eadyyl, Adriana dedicated herself to maintaining the deserted groves and shrines. They worked unmolested since the invaders eschewed the forest they feared, and when Adriana grew to womanhood, she chose as her patron Rache, the Goddess of Revenge. Dedicating herself to the service of the Goddess, she set up abode at Rache's sacred springs. Adriana lived alone, contented, gathering sweet buds in spring, berries in summer, and nuts when the leaves turned brown. She kept a flock of wild goats and a clutch of hens that had wandered from an abandoned farm. She lived in seclusion, avoiding the Astrians unless she wanted prey.

She found them pitifully easy to snare. With magick and wiles, she lured them into her woods, and after wielding the power she drew from Rache, she ensnared them. She left them lost and wandering, forever shadows of the arrogant men who had stumbled into her domain.

And now another victim approached, oblivious to his role as sacrifice. The lone horseman rode across the distant meadows. Adriana had planned on setting fern spores around the cool spring today, but that could wait. Rache preferred prey to planting.

From her perch on the escarpment, Adriana drew from the springs below and wove a mist, snaking it toward the meadows and the narrow track. She wanted the rider to wander off the main bridleway toward Rache's altar. As the mist swirled thicker and stronger, Adriana pulled out her flute and played a silent song to the rider's mount. Lured by the calming music, the confused animal veered his way toward the forest and the sacred springs.

CR SO

Mark of Windhaw thanked the Five Gods he wasn't a superstitious man. Else he'd be convinced this mission was bedeviled. Two sennights ago, three of them had left Astria at the emperor's behest. One of four parties sent to the new territories to investigate reports of abuses and mistreatment of the subject peoples. Mark hoped the other three envoys had fared better. His recorder had broken his leg when his mount had stumbled and fallen in a hidden badger trap as they took a shortcut across a fallow meadow. Karrel now lay in a village inn at Four Cross, his leg splinted. His mount had been less fortunate, so Mark had sent Pait, his squire, back to the nearest barracks with a request for remounts while he journeyed on to Merridale, the first town on his circuit.

If the fine weather continued, Mark hoped to arrive in less than two days' ride, but the sudden onset of mist meant delay. Of necessity he slowed, staying on the marked trail to avoid misdirection, but letting Rian, his mount, set the pace. It was an inconvenience, nothing more. He carried the emperor's sigil. Not even in these barbaric lands would anyone dare hinder his progress.

He hated these fogs! One lost all sense of time and distance in the dank silence. He'd been alone on the road for most of the day, but had at least seen his way. Now his only hope was to stay on the trail until the blasted fog cleared. Rian was content, more than content in fact, as she gamely clopped on. Mark sensed she was willing to proceed faster, but he kept a tight hold on the reins. After Karrel's mishap, he rode cautiously.

After a time, Mark sensed the mist thinning. The ground, though still well-worn, looked rocky beneath Rian's hooves. Around him, Mark noticed the outlines of dark trees and the distant sound of water. A river perhaps? The Merri even? If so, he was nearer his destination than he had expected. It was unlikely given his setbacks, more likely a stream or brook. As the mist thinned more, Mark sensed the incline of the path and noticed more trees. Had he wandered into the forest? Rian's hooves sounded on rock, not trodden earth, but the path was firm and dry, and Mark gave his mount her head. She moved faster until, as if bursting from the cloying damp, they emerged above the mist into warm spring sunshine.

They were on a rocky knoll in a forest clearing. Ahead of them was the stream he'd heard for the past while. They must have followed the path uphill and now stood just armspans

17

from where the water sprang from the escarpment. Mark dismounted and led Rian to the water's edge. While she drank, he looked around and listened. There was not a soul in sight, but his senses alerted him to a watcher—the mists still clinging to the trees could conceal a rebel army. He rested his hand on his sword hilt, but nothing broke the silence except the jangle of Rian's bridle and the sound of rushing water.

Mark knelt on the rocks by the stream bank and filled his waterleathers, drank deeply, then refilled them. He cupped his hands to scoop up the clear water and washed his face and neck. He dried them on the lining of his cloak. Refreshed, he stood up and looked around. There had to be another river, a waterfall even. This stream burbled over the rocks and gravel, but from nearby came a roar of a torrent. He felt no desire to explore; this little sun-drenched corner was haven enough. He'd wait for the fog to clear completely and proceed on his way. Rian seemed content to chomp the wide verge of new grass that bordered the stream.

Cloaking herself with invisibility, Adriana watched her prey.

He was travel-stained, and his rough-coated horse in no better condition. The animal hesitated, perhaps sensing the magick around, but her rider had no such qualms. After he finished drinking, he stood up and brushed his hood off his face. The sunlight caught golden lights in his long hair. A yellow-haired invader. The worst kind. The dark-haired mercenaries came, killed and returned to their own country. But the yellow-haired invaders stayed, taking lands and farms from the vanquished and inhabiting the houses of those they had murdered. Whole families of invaders now lived in Endholm, the village she'd fled those years ago. The invaders' slaves farmed the fields her slain uncles had planted with roots and grain.

18

After drinking and washing, her prey led his horse over to the swathe of new grass. He patted the beast's neck and talked to it, showing more concern for a horse than Astrians usually showed villagers and children. No matter, the invader had drunk from Rache's cool water; soon he would pay the debt for which Adriana yearned.

She eased down from her perch, stepping forward as the stranger raised his foot to the stirrup.

"Sir Traveler," she said. "Welcome to Rache's springs. Will you not stay a little and rest? Your horse looks tired, and the road ahead is hard and perilous in the mist."

Turning, hand on sword, he looked at her, his eyes wrinkling at the corners as he smiled. To her utter surprise, he inclined his head in courtesy. "Lady, forgive the intrusion. I was lost in the mist when I spied this stream and paused to refresh myself. I thought this glade abandoned." His eyes shone blue as periwinkles in spring.

"Not abandoned, traveler." She smiled and took a deliberate step forward. "I live here."

"Alone, lady? Is that wise? These are hard and dangerous times."

"Indeed, they are." She fought to keep the irony from her voice. "But I have lived here alone for years and nothing ill has befallen me."

"And I, lady, trust and pray it never does. There have been ill times enough."

It pained her to agree with an enemy, so she inclined her head, and on meeting those clear eyes again proposed, "I have little to offer but Rache's clear water, sweetberries and roasted roots, but if you would accept my woodland hospitality…"

He hesitated, but his hand hung clear of his sword hilt. In his arrogance, he considered a mere woman no threat.

19

Adriana smiled. "Come, and let us sit in the sunshine." She indicated the flat rocks that served her as table and bench.

As he met her gaze, she willed hunger and weariness on him and watched the debate behind his eyes. He was uncertain, and she smiled to calm his unease. "I would be honored. I have but few visitors."

"Lady, if I do not intrude, then I gladly accept your hospitality." He stepped forward, and Adriana knew he was hers as surely as any mayfly caught in a spider's web. "I have food aplenty and invite you to dine with me," he said.

He took a pouch from his saddle and added his provisions to her roasted roots and berries. While Adriana brought drinking vessels and bowls from the depths of her cave, he produced ham—from some dispossessed peasant's hogs no doubt—cheese and a hunk of dry, but still sweet, dark bread. She hadn't tasted oven-baked wheaten bread in years. Just looking at it, she smelled new-baked loaves coming from Fax the Baker's oven. Enough! No time for daydreaming. Adriana smiled at the intruder as he sliced ham and placed it on a trencher of bread. She offered him a treen dish of roasted roots.

"Lady, as your guest, I must identify myself and my house. I am Mark of Windhaw, son of the lines of Dingle and Saltram."

How the invaders spoke of bloodlines and manors, as if property and possessions were all important. "I am Adriana."

"No patronymic or distaff name, Lady Adriana?"

She shook her head. "I have no family, and..." she smiled, letting her mouth curve just enough to set the dimple in her left cheek, "in the woods, we lay no claim to titles." She took, with both hands, the trencher he offered. The ham was pink and moist, no doubt fresh-cured this past winter. Her mouth watered at the thought of the taste of salt and rich meat. Never before had a victim offered her food, and she half-hesitated, but the smell of fresh ham was too much to resist. "I have nothing this rich to offer. Here in the woods, we live on berries in the summer, nuts in the autumn and stored roots through the winter."

"Lady, in this glade, and with such company, all is a banquet." The corners of his blue eyes crinkled as he smiled and reached for a roasted parsnip. A pretty enemy in looks and words.

As he bit into the dark, roasted root, Adriana tasted the ham. It was as she remembered—salty, moist, and needing chewing. The taste evoked memories and times long gone, of winter festivals, spring plantings, harvest homes and sacred feasts—a world long bled away under the invaders' swords.

Her victim was hungry, that was clear, but he ate with grace and skill, closing his mouth as he chewed and cutting food into small portions before spearing them with the point of his knife. Even his beard stayed clean as he ate. A gracious and dainty invader who smiled as he sliced her parsnips and took the treen jug himself to the stream to refill it.

It would be no hardship to seduce Mark of Windhaw.

Adriana watched as he bent to dip the wooden jug in the sparkling waters. He'd discarded his cloak to reveal his dark shirt and riding breeches, which only served to emphasize the breadth of his shoulders and the strength in his legs. Invaders never had bowed legs from famine and disease. Although invaders seldom acted with such courtesy, or walked with such grace. She made herself watch the afternoon sun glitter on the ripples of Rache's stream, not on the handsome Astrian picking purple water daisies. As he bent, the leather of his breeches strained against the muscles of his thighs. As he stood, she tore a crust of sweet dark bread and chewed. Hunger assuaged, soon it would be time to tempt other appetites.

Her Astrian prey offered her the posy of daisies with a bow. "Little enough thanks, Lady Adriana, for your graciousness...but I travel on the emperor's charge, and I fear am unprepared for such hospitality as yours."

How truly right. "The emperor sent you alone into his conquered territories?" Or was Mark of Windhaw the herald of another invasion?

He sat down gracefully, tucking one booted foot under and stretching out his other leg. "I didn't set out alone on my commission. Misfortune befell us. I'm one of the emperor's auditors. I had a recorder and a page when I set out." He told her of their misadventures.

"What will you do without them? It's unsafe in wild parts for lone travelers." Most unsafe! They fell into Rache's clutches.

His broad shoulders rose and fell as his wide mouth curled at the corners. "I carry the emperor's sigil. Few would risk his anger. I left Karrel under that protection at an inn, to rest until he can ride, and I hope to meet Pait and new mounts when I reach Merridale."

Merridale—the nearest market town, where her uncles had once sold lambs and pigs, and her mother had traded eggs and honey fruit. In those distant times, market days had been like festivals. "And from Merridale you travel farther?"

"Perhaps. I will stay there as long as necessary to fulfill the emperor's orders. If there is time before winter descends, I go on to Stoneholm and Holmhaven, but I will not leave Merridale until satisfied."

"Why did he send you?" Was she asking too much? It was of no consequence why this invader was here.

"He has heard stories of misuse and abuse since he annexed these lands." Mark shook his head. "I am sent to ascertain the truth and ensure peace and law."

Indeed! "It has been many years. Why wait this long? Is he not satisfied with his appointed masters?" They'd compelled the emperor's law with horrendous zeal.

"Lady, here in this sylvan paradise I doubt the affairs of state intrude." Was he foolish or merely ignorant? "The last years have been hard on the empire." Harder still on the vanquished. "Now that all is stable in the realm and the threats to the throne removed, the emperor wishes to ensure peace and justice throughout the empire."

"He believes there is injustice?"

"There are tales. I come to ascertain the truth."

And she could tell him hard ones, but what would it matter? Did he really believe his emperor cared about mere peasants? She'd seen otherwise. It was time to appease Rache.

Adriana took a sip of water and let the cool liquid play on her tongue. She then focused her power to weave a spell of weariness. Mark of Windhaw yawned, covering his mouth with the back of his callused hand.

"Your pardon, Lady Adriana, I fear weariness overcomes me."

"Small surprise, sir, if you have ridden since sun up and through the mist. If you will, you may rest in my shelter."

"Lady, you are ever gracious. To stay would be a pleasure, but my duty to my emperor calls."

Forest magick called louder. At his next yawn, his eyes closed, his long, honey-colored lashes brushed his cheeks before he forced his eyes open again. "I must..." He stood, feet unsteady and eyelids heavy with her spell.

Adriana sprung up beside him, grasping his upper arm with both hands. His muscles warmed under her fingers as she led him into her cave. Guiding his stumbling steps toward the sleeping pallet in the corner, she eased him to the ground. He was deep asleep as she covered him with sleeping furs.

Adriana stood up and glanced down at the sleeping warrior—or auditor as he called himself. His chin bore a scar that had surely been acquired in battle, and his body was strong as a fighter's. He was pretty though, his hair golden against the dark furs, and his skin weather-tanned to the color of ripened waynuts. A fine sacrifice to Rache.

Chapter Two

Adriana lingered just a little, watching the flutter of his eyelashes and listening to the soft brush of his breath between his full lips. In repose, a gentleness settled on his features. Awake, he'd shown a courtesy and courtliness she'd not expected. Strange for an Astrian to seem so...civilized. The others had been rough or arrogant. Seducing and ensnaring them had been a duty. With Mark of Windhaw, it would be no hardship.

An impatient whinny brought her back to her task. While they ate, his horse had roamed loose, but now it seemed she had wandered uphill and was pawing the rocks and sparse turf outside the cave.

The beast was not easy to calm, as if she sensed the magick around her, but under Adriana's hands and voice, she let herself be unsaddled and led into the forest. Returning to the shrine, Adriana sorted through Mark of Windhaw's belongings. Aside from clean linen and necessities for travel across the country, he carried a quantity of paper and pens and a large bundle of notes in scrolls and packets. It seemed he had spoken truthfully about being an auditor. He had a little gold in his pockets, but in the pouch on his saddle, she found two large leather bags holding more gold than she'd seen in her entire life. She debated throwing them in the river, but put them aside. Here in the forest she had no use for Astrian gold, but who knew, one day? Buried in the earth at the back of her cavern it would not go to enrich her family's killers.

Later she would sort his belongings into those of use and those to be useful as fuel or to trade. She moved everything out of sight and climbed behind the rocks to wash in the warm spring, carrying with her enough furs and drying cloths for later.

CR ℘

Mark of Windhaw was still deep in Adriana's enchanted sleep when she returned. She stood in the mouth of her cave and watched his chest rise and fall under the fur covers. He was so handsome in repose, it seemed almost a shame to ensnare him. What! Was she wavering in mind and mission? Mark of Windhaw was Astrian—enemy, destroyer and rapist. Physical beauty concealing the human rot within.

She would not falter. Her oath and her dedication would shore up her will. He was fair to the eyes. What matter? Duty, welcome or unwelcome, was still duty, and she would not fail. She stepped into the cave, knelt by Mark of Windhaw's sleeping body and pulled back the sleeping furs.

She'd be as blind as old Meg from back in her long-destroyed village to miss the strength of his body beneath the leather breeches and black woolen tunic. The lacing of his tunic had come undone, revealing the white linen shirt beneath and a glimpse of male chest. His breeches fit like a second skin, accentuating the strength in his thighs and the length of his legs. One arm was stretched out toward the wall, the other rested on his chest. His fingers were long and the nails neatly trimmed, his hands hard. Not callused as a carpenter or a

26

farmer, but neither soft like one of the invading priests. She rested her hand on his, the tips of her fingers only reaching to his knuckles. Yes! Mark of Windhaw was a large man—would his cock be in proportion to the rest of him?

Soon she'd find out.

But first she had to wake him.

She walked over to the cool spring and took a deep drink of water, cooling her lips and mouth before returning to where Mark of Windhaw still slumbered. Brushing the dark gold hair off his forehead, she looked down at his face, handsome and relaxed, a slight smile curving his mouth. He smelled of fresh air and man and the slight trace of horse. He was indeed a finely built male—lean and firm of body, and most pleasing to the eye. Truly, a worthy sacrifice.

Smiling, Adriana kissed him on his eyelids. As she sat back on her heels, her hand on his shoulder, he opened his eyes. Surprise, confusion and sudden awareness all flickered in his deep blue eyes.

"Lady," he said, looking around the cave. "I thought I was dreaming."

"Not dreaming, Mark of Windhaw. You are my guest. And I offer you the hospitality of Rache." The hand on his shoulder eased toward his open shirt. "Seldom do I have company, and I would welcome you in Rache's name."

"Is this seemly, lady?" he asked, his hand coming as if to move hers, but instead covering her fingers with his.

"Why not, sir? Would you refuse me this courtesy?" As she spoke, her free hand traced the open neck of his shirt, loosed the lacings a little more and brushed the golden curls on his chest. "I am much alone, sir. Your company honors me, and I crave your generosity."

"Lady..." he began, but her lips stopped his objection with a slow and measured kiss.

Mark of Windhaw was a strong man, but not made of iron. She noticed with satisfaction as his breath caught and his chest rose and fell. "Will you not stay awhile, sir? Is it not unchivalrous to refuse a lady's request?"

"Indeed, lady, it is. I must not so offend." He pulled her to him and kissed her full on the mouth.

He was the epitome of gentleness—his mouth warm against her cool one. His touch soft as he pressed his lips on hers, making no effort to push or hasten—just satisfied, it seemed, to caress her lips with his. Sweet, short kisses that stirred her mind but never forced. Light brushes of skin as he kissed her upper and lower lips alternately, as his hands tunneled through her hair, his fingertips stroking her scalp with the lightest of touches. Her heart fluttered against her ribs, her breath caught in tempo with his touch. There was no haste, no push, no demand, just a gentle possession that had her yearning for more.

No! She led. She seduced. He was usurping her role. It was wrong. It was wonderful. It was not as it should be.

She had to regain control, but his lips brushed her chin, the curve of her cheeks and edge of her mouth before coming back to claim her lips with his. Her mind buzzed with desire. Why fight it? Was this not what she wanted? Mark of Windhaw willing and aroused? She joined in the kiss, pressing her lips to his, working his mouth with hers, welcoming his tongue as her hands eased inside his shirt to stroke the warm flesh and to feel the flutter of his heart under her fingertips.

At last he broke the kiss, lifting his mouth off hers. "Sweet Lady Adriana. I know not who you are, but the Five Gods were good when they guided my steps to your abode."

"Mayhap 'twas the Goddess who led you here," she suggested.

He stared. "Lady, you follow the pagan ways?"

"Why would I not? In the woods, we have little use for your harsh religion. Many years ago, I dedicated myself to Rache. I am her priestess, and this," she indicated the cave around, and the stream and grass beyond the opening, "is her shrine. Do you think ill of it...or me?" She watched as conflicting thoughts battered each other behind his blue eyes.

"I think," he said, "you are the most beautiful creature in this world. I have found you and would make you mine."

Precisely what she planned. He'd never forget her—no matter how much he willed it. "Let us become each other's inspiration."

"Dear lady! They told me strange things awaited within the New Territories. They knew not half the truth."

"You find me strange?"

"Magnificently so! To discover such beauty in the deep forest far exceeds anything I expected. But to find such beauty in the guise of pagan priestess..." He shook his head.

"Did they tell you we were crones and hags?" The look on his face answered that. She leaned over and kissed his cheek, brushing her hand over his chest. She left her hand on his chest as she drew back from the kiss, but his hand cupped the back of her head and drew her close.

She let him turn her face to take her mouth with his—she expected this. How many times had it been now? Each one the same to the end. Mark of Windhaw was falling into place as her next prize, but as he pressed forward, his mouth possessing hers, his hands stroking her hair, a strange awareness filled her mind. She leaned close, wanting, needing to feel his strength and presence. He kissed slowly, as if tasting her lips, his hands smoothing her head and shoulders.

Her mind stirred at this touch and the sweet seduction of his kisses. With gentle insistence, he pulled her against him, drawing her alongside him. She nestled close, as much to feel his tenderness and strength as to familiarize herself with the body she'd soon possess. Her hand stroked his thigh, feeling the strength of his muscle under the leather breeches and slowly she inched her fingers toward the tented leather at his groin. He needed her, and soon, she'd take his power and his mind. Meanwhile, his kisses and embrace delighted her.

His hand trailed over her neck and shoulder to cup her breast. She heard a little whimper in a space beyond her head. Not his, but surely not hers? She shivered with anticipation as he moved to caress her other breast, her mind racing along with her pulse and her heart. This was all wrong, but all wonderful. She pressed closer. Never had she felt this heat, this need, this distraction. She pulled back, gently, so as not to anger or alert him.

They watched each other. Was her skin as flushed as his? Her eyes as dark? Her breath as ragged? Impossible! She drew her strength from Rache. Adriana always controlled, and now, as the heat of his kisses abated, she regained her composure. That embrace was an aberration, nothing more.

"Sweet Adriana, for a kiss such as yours, I would have crossed the three deserts and scaled every mountain in the empire. You are a man's dream, come to life in the wild lands."

"I was waiting here until you came," she replied, her self-command restored now that she had put distance between them. Rache's waters would calm her and help her focus her mind. Adriana had seen many times what warm water and sweet magick did to men. She stood and held out her hand. "Sweet traveler, you have fed and rested—why not bathe?"

He stood, running his hands through his golden hair and flexing his broad shoulders. "Lady, you are gracious beyond words. And cool water will refresh." He took a step toward the cavern's opening.

"No, Mark of Windhaw. Rache has two springs—one for drinking and one for bathing." She closed her hand over his. "Come with me."

CR ℘

"You've questioned the urchin?" Quel of Woldene, acting commander of Fort Antin, looked across the table at his major.

"We have, sir. Thoroughly."

Quel nodded. He knew exactly how thorough Den Morton could be—that was why he'd picked him for the work. "You're certain he's not lying?"

"No one lies after my questioning."

True. "Bring him in." Though, drag him in was more probable—scarce likelihood the lad could still stand. But he'd served his purpose, and if what Den said were true, it had been fortuitous beyond words that the boy had chosen this fort to beg for succor. And begging he'd been, ever since he'd shown them the emperor's sigil.

The lad staggered in and collapsed at Quel's feet as the guards released him. Den *had* been thorough. Two swollen and bloodied eyes looked up at Quel. The bleeding mouth rasped, "Sir, I came for succor in the emperor's name. Why have your men used me thus?"

Silly fool, had he not yet realized? Quel had to smile. "Foolish lad, in these wild parts, we are far from the emperor's hand." And his weakness. They hadn't subdued these wild lands with philosophy and education, and if this sniveling boy were a product of the emperor's enlightenment, Quel would fight to preserve the ways he knew. "We do not take kindly to interference on the frontier."

"I come in the emperor's name, bearing his sigil."

He still didn't understand. "Yes, and now I hold that sigil." Shock flickered in one almost-open eye. "Thanks to your assistance, we know where and how to detain his auditor. Your injured companion died in his bed in the Inn at Four Cross and soon there will be none to carry tales back to Astria."

Fear, shock and horror registered across the battered face. The lad really had loved his master. How pathetically foolish! Look where loyalty got him. If he'd given the information when first demanded, he'd have died swiftly. For his intransigence, he now lay in agony from ripped-out toenails, burned feet and crippled hands.

"What shall we do with him?" Den asked. "Throw him down the cistern?"

Quel looked down at the crumpled lad. Even now, the battered face and swollen eyes begged for mercy. "Sir, have pity..." he mumbled from his swollen jaw.

"No, Den." The boy looked up in hope. Foolish child. "I want to say the lad came and I sent him on his way accompanied by soldiers." Den grinned, the lad looked merely perplexed. "Make up a party of volunteers, have them take him into the forest and leave him." He smiled down at the now panic-stricken eyes. "The forest animals will finish your job for you and leave no trace and no witness."

The lad was sobbing as they dragged him away.

Quel vaguely wondered whom Den would press into venturing into the forest. Convicts from the pound no doubt— soldiers desperate enough to risk the dreaded forest for the chance to escape the noose. The acting commander sat down behind his desk and stared at the yellowed walls. Life was full of opportunities if a man quashed his scruples. Quel had discarded his many years ago.

He hated these wild lands and feared the savages. They needed containing, and force was the only way. He thought briefly of the lad now condemned to die in the forest, and at considerable length of the use he could make of his information. Quel smiled as he raised an inkstick and penned a letter to the governor of Merridale. A letter marked with the emperor's sigil would never be disbelieved. Life brought rewards to the bold and devious.

Chapter Three

"Lady, where are you leading us?"

Adriana smiled over her shoulder. Mark of Windhaw was half-enraptured already. "To Rache's other spring," she replied, leading him across the cavern to a tunnel in the far wall. As she stepped out of the short tunnel into sunlight, she turned to watch his face. Barbarians were always astounded to find this temple in the middle of savage forest.

Mark of Windhaw was no different.

He stopped in the tunnel opening and stared. Blue eyes widening, he scanned the high stone walls, the smooth paving under his feet, the carved basin under the spring and the stone-rimmed bathing cistern beneath. But most of all, he gaped at the steam that rose from the water. Stepping forward, he ran his strong hand through the cascade that poured over the rim of the basin into the cistern.

He looked around with increased wonder. "Lady, what is this place?"

"Rache's warm spring. This is where I bathe."

"A wonder indeed. I have heard talk of hot springs emerging from deep in the earth, but thought them wild romancing."

"No, sir." She took a step closer. "There are five shrines where warm water rises, each is dedicated to one of the Goddesses. This is Rache's."

"But who built this?"

"Ancients long gone—those who respected and worshiped Rache." Not exactly true, Eadwyn had said it was a ruin long before Rache's women restored and dedicated it to their use. But what would an Astrian know or care? They destroyed. They did not build.

Mark of Windhaw turned and walked around the rim of the cistern, pausing at intervals to examine stonework or inspect the carving in the high walls. He ran his strong hands over the finely hewn stones and shook his head. Adriana watched, trying hard to ignore the sunlight on his hair and the look of wonder and interest in his face.

"Lady Adriana," he said, his voice seeming tight and drawn. "What a pity it is this skill was lost. Buildings such as this could last ages."

"This shrine has lasted ages," she said. "None remember the building of it."

He nodded. "If only these ways were still known!" He sighed. "One of my commissions from the emperor is to find a site for a university. If we could erect a building such as this, it would be a shrine to knowledge."

"What is a university? A place to train priests?" They needed no more of them. She'd already seen what they could do.

"More than that. A seat of learning open to all scholars. There is knowledge in these lands, old lore and wisdom, that is passing away. We would keep it alive."

It would be better to keep people alive! All this talk was delaying her purpose. She walked back to where he stood by

35

the carved rim of the basin. "I did not bring you here to marvel at masonry or discourse on old lore. Warm water is for bathing, Mark of Windhaw, and you have traveled far."

They were not quite touching, but she felt the heat of his body and smelled male sweat and horse. Yes, he did need to bathe. It was the best prelude to seduction she knew. The warm water would loosen his muscles and his will. This was a duty she'd long accepted, but for once she approached it without dread. She stepped closer and, standing on tiptoe, kissed him on the lips.

To her astonishment, he stepped back, his eyes wide. "Lady!"

His shock amused her. "Sir?" She tilted her head and stepped back. "I've angered you?"

"No, lady, but this is not..."

"Not what?"

"Not seemly!"

"You did not repulse my embrace before."

"It is not your embrace, lady. Your graciousness and hospitality honor me, but to bathe like this is unseemly."

She wrinkled her nose. "Washed guests are a courtesy to all."

He colored under the weathered tan. "Lady, I would not offend after your generosity."

Smiling, she purposely and deliberately eyed him, from sleep-rumpled hair to his leather boots, and everywhere in between. Her glance discomfited him. No matter. She reached out her hand, and this time, his fingers closed over hers. "Sir, our customs may not be yours, but would you forbid me to observe Rache's obligations of hospitality?"

"Lady, never would I wish you forsworn."

"Then come and bathe." She stepped away, pausing on the rim of the bathing basin just long enough to draw her robe and shift over her head. She sensed his gaze boring down her spine, then she turned just enough to offer him a glimpse of breast before sitting on the edge and sliding into the warm water.

Her gasp of pleasure was no act. She loved the caress of water against her body, the wash of warmth over her breasts and the sensation between her legs as she leveled on her belly to kick away from the rim. After a few strokes, she looked back. Her quarry still waited, feet planted on the rock, legs apart and hands on hips.

He was resisting, but not for long. Not the way his gaze burned down at her. His restraint intrigued her. He was the first victim ever to hesitate at the sight of her nakedness. Some had even jumped in clothed. One almost drowned with his boots still on.

Adriana stood and turned to face him. She deliberately brushed the water off her arms and breasts.

No man had ever resisted her and Mark of Windhaw was no different from the rest. He was sitting on a ledge pulling off his second boot. It took mere moments to strip off his tunic and breeches. Her breath caught as she watched him pull his shirt over his head. Sweet Rache! He was beautiful—his broad chest almost golden in the sunlight, and his legs planted surely and confidently on the paved way.

He took a few steps back, ran forward, then jumped. The swell washed water over her breasts in a warm rush. Time to meet him.

She dived under the still-rippling water and stroked toward him, breaking the surface an arm's length away. Shaking her wet hair from her face, she smiled and held out her hand. "Come, Mark of Windhaw."

"You observe outrageous courtesies in the forest, Lady Adriana."

"I would offer you all our courtesies, sir. Let Rache's waters soothe your aches and ease the strain of travel."

"And you, Lady Adriana, what would you do?" His chest rose and fell, the sunlight glinting on the warm drops that rolled down his chest and arms.

"What you desire the most."

"You can read my thoughts, lady?"

"I can read desire in your eyes, Mark of Windhaw. I have few riches and fewer belongings, but I can offer the hospitality of one who dedicates herself to Rache." As she smiled, she drew heat from the water and willed it into his flesh. Soon she'd see his defenses crumble. He wanted her, that was clear, but still he hesitated. "You find me unpleasing?"

He chuckled at that. "Never, lady... Your beauty amazes and your generosity astounds. I am unfamiliar with your ways and hesitate lest I offend."

"The only offense to Rache is hesitation. A slight to one of her dedicated servants would be insult indeed."

"Never!" He crossed the gap between them and, to her surprise, made the first move. Gathering her to him, holding her tight against his hard body—his hard aroused body, she noticed with satisfaction—he whispered, "Lady Adriana, I have heard tales of enchantment and magick in these far lands. Have you enchanted me?"

"Not yet." She tilted her head and smiled.

His mouth came down on hers—hot, urgent and gentle. He opened her lips and pressed his tongue against hers, caressing and stroking with heated, fevered moves as she leaned ever closer, pressing into his growing erection. For a moment, she was lost between the heat of his embrace and the warmth of the water lapping against them. She rocked her hips, sending warm waves rippling between their legs and eliciting a quiet moan from Mark of Windhaw.

Or was the moan hers? It could not be! A mere echo off the rock walls around. "Come deeper, sir." She led him into the center of the pool. Here she was out of her depth so she floated on her back, parting her legs and looking up at the sky. It was well toward sunset, but still warm; in this sheltered grotto they could sport till dusk. By then he would be hers. Adriana sighed. He was handsome, fine of body and face, but she would not let a fair face blind her mission. A handsome man was a better offering on the altar of revenge than an ugly one, and to ensnare a man so close to the emperor who'd wrought such ill...

Turning onto her belly, she looked over her shoulder at Mark. "On the ledge opposite, I have white sand to wash with."

She didn't watch to see if he followed. No need. She heard the splash as his arms broke the water, and sensed the pull as he followed close behind.

She'd almost forgotten he was still wearing his underbreeches, but as they stepped out of the water, she noticed that he might just as well have been naked. Wet linen clung to his well-muscled thighs and tented over his erection.

She scooped up a handful of fine sand and knelt. "Come closer, Mark of Windhaw." He stood over her, his erection level with her eyes. As she watched, his hard belly rose and fell with each speeding breath. His need was all too apparent. Satisfaction was at hand. When had she ever failed? "It is our way of hospitality to those who honor us with their visits."

"You are not my servant, or my page."

"No, I am a priestess offering service. I entreat you, accept this, or Rache will consider I've failed." She rested her hand on the damp linen plastered to his thigh. "Kneel, Mark of Windhaw."

He knelt.

Moving behind him, she gently massaged his back, rubbing the sand across his broad shoulders and down the valley of his spine. She spread her fingers wide, kneading and pressing to ease the tension in his muscles. She worked gently over the scar on his shoulder. No doubt that was acquired when ravaging her lands or maiming her people, but nonetheless she eased her fingertips over the proud flesh, stroking the hardened weal. When he gave a soft sigh, she paused to drop a kiss on one rounded shoulder. Yes, a fine-bodied male was a truly pleasing sight, and none she'd yet encountered matched Mark of Windhaw for male beauty...and courtesy. Some had leapt on her flesh and taken her with haste, but this time, it would be a pleasing enchantment.

She eased her fingertips inside the band of his underbreeches, then withdrew, but not before pausing to appreciate his firm rear and fine thighs. She gently stroked one cheek of his backside before moving around to face him. Smiling up at him, she reached to scoop up another handful of sand, but he moved faster.

"I would dishonor my house if I did not meet hospitality with courtesy," he said, reaching down and holding up his hand, the soft sand trickling though his fingers. "Let us bathe each other."

No one had ever offered that...but what was the harm? She turned, presenting her back to him, and idly wondered how she appeared to him. Was her skin smooth? Did her back curve like his? His hips were firm and narrow, not rounded like hers. Her belly was softer, her hands smaller...but her strength and purpose were great. She was a dedicated priestess. He was...

"How feels that, Lady Adriana?" he asked, brushing sand over her back.

"Like lying on the sand in summertime."

"And this?" His hands stroked her shoulders, his fingertips caressing the upper swell of her breasts.

She sighed.

His hands came under her breasts, cupping their fullness.

She leaned forward, pressing her breasts into his hands, closing her eyes as his fingertips brushed her nipples. She let the pleasure of his touch and closeness wash over her like a summer breeze.

How right she'd been! This time was like no other. His lips brushed the side of her neck, and she whimpered with delight at the wild sensations such a gentle caress released. By Rache! It was wonderful! A gentle warmth seeped through her flesh as he whispered, "Lady, does that please you?"

They both knelt up as they scooped handful after handful of fine white sand and rubbed each other's body clean. His body was as fine as any she'd seen. His skin was warm and smooth under her fingers, his nipples hardening like young buds. She ran her fingers down his torso, relishing the feel of muscle under warm skin. Auditor he might call himself, but this was no soft-bodied clerk who spent his life indoors scribbling with inksticks.

Her hands trailed down strong thighs, skirting his erection behind the damp linen. Without hesitating, she loosed the tapes fastening his underbreeches. They fell open, revealing a firm, smooth cock rising hard from the nest of golden curls. Beauteous indeed. Adriana longed to wrap her fingers around his cock and feel his warmth and male strength—soon. Time enough for everything. Why spoil the present pleasantness with duty? She stood and looked up at him. A feast for the eyes in truth—what a tragedy he was Astrian!

But nonetheless, they had time and opportunity to prolong this play and she would take whatever pleasure her onerous oaths permitted.

"I think, Mark of Windhaw, it would serve us to bathe now." She walked over to the rim of the basin. Looking back at him— tall, beauteous and fine to behold—she slipped into the warm water with a sigh. She ducked under and broke the surface several armspans away. Standing, she brushed her hair off her face and scooped up water to rinse off the last traces of sand.

Mark of Windhaw was nowhere to be seen! She turned fast, the water eddying around her in ripples. Where was he? Surely he could not have fled. The tunnel was across the pool, and his clothes still lay in the heap where he'd discarded them. He would not leave naked. Had he drowned in the water? That thought brought moisture to her eyes. No! Her mind screamed in silent disappointment. Not dead! Not that fine and handsome body.

Her concern was nonsense! What if Rache's waters claimed him before she, Adriana, had wrought just vengeance? It was all one offering, one sacrifice. But oh! Adriana's heart clenched. It was too soon...he should have been hers first, but Rache had chosen, it seemed...

Best accept the Goddess's will.

The water muffled Adriana's scream as her feet were pulled from under her. She reached out to grab the arms around her legs, clutching at flesh and hair as they rose to the surface together. Mark of Windhaw had her by the waist. They were chest-to-chest and face-to-face, and before she caught enough breath to protest, his mouth came down, and words and recriminations became superfluous.

By Rache! Never in all her born days had Adriana know such heady pleasure. It was not just his mouth on hers, or his tongue teasing and caressing, but also the way his hands clasped her waist and drew her close.

"Sweet lady," he whispered, lifting his mouth off hers for a breath space, "I would have wandered the woods forever to find you!"

Her heart caught, and it was not just at the trail of kisses down her neck. How close to the truth he'd spoken! Soon he would wander the woods in discontent and regret, but now was not the time to dwell on her future duty. Best to dwell on his arms strong around her as he lifted her out of the water and fastened his mouth on her breast.

She cried out in joy, surprise and sensual yearning. How could a man, and an Astrian at that, do this to her? How could she permit him to stop?

As his mouth moved to her other nipple, she leaned back in his arms and let her mind float free. Wild longings stirred deep in her soul as her body ached for more. She did not understand this, but had no need to. It was beyond reason. Her mind closed to all but desire for his touch and need for his kisses. Duty awaited, but for now she'd lose herself in these new joys.

He lowered her down his body, his erection hard against her belly. "Sweet Adriana," his voice came tight and deep. "There is magick in this place." How right he was. "Your magick and your loving. How I bless the mist that made me lose my way and find you." His hands brushed her shoulders. "There's still sand on your skin."

Her hand came up his chest. "And on you. Come." Her arm around his waist, they walked toward the waterfall and stood together under the warm cascade. They let the flowing water wash their bodies clean. More was unnecessary, the rush of water was enough to sweep the last vestiges of sand from their bodies, but Adriana couldn't keep her hands still. They itched to slide over Mark's hard, warm flesh and the golden hair that now lay smooth and flat. She indulged that need, trailing fingertips over his shoulders and down his chest, pausing over his nipples that rose like dark buds against his fair skin.

Remembering the pleasure his lips had given, she bent her head, first licking his nipple before taking it between her lips. As it hardened even more under her tongue, he clasped the back of her head in his hands.

"Sweetness, indeed!" he said. "You are my utter temptation."

She was snared between pleasure and satisfaction. He was hers, beyond all doubt, but equally sure was the unexpected promise of pleasure. She looked up into eyes, blue as the sky above, that glimmered like sunlight as he looked at her.

"If you would permit, lady..." One hand cupped her breast, his other her rump, pulling her closer. "There is much I would do to show you loving."

"Why should I not permit? I offered my hospitality, sir."

His wide lips parted as if to reply, but she stood on tiptoe and pulled his head down. This time she kissed, willing desire, need and abandon into him. Time to take this further, but Mark of Windhaw was content for now, and strangely, so was she.

Hand in hand, they swam to the middle of the pool, splashing and playing like water bears. Touching, diving and circling, stopping to kiss and caress each other, then parting to dive and turn.

This was pleasure! But she had a duty. Not wanting to break the mood, but knowing Rache demanded more than play, Adriana swam to the far edge where she'd spread the furs and covers.

Mark of Windhaw followed.

He stayed close in her wake. When she lowered her feet to the bottom and turned, he was there—warm water beading on his chest, smiling in a way that set her senses awash with desire and confusion.

They stood thigh-deep in water and she'd be made of stone not to want her fill of the sight before her eyes. Clothed in nothing but sunlight and warm water, Mark of Windhaw smiled. And waited, watching her as if she brought his dreams to life. His needs were evident in the heat in his eyes and the cock that stood hard and high, pointing straight at her as if to indicate the target of his desire.

It was the self-same desire that poured through her, bathing her skin with need and her mind with an urgency she barely comprehended. What was it about this man that stirred her so? Never before had she felt this heat within, this longing for his body on hers. The yearning for his cock deep within her, to hold him close and satisfy his need with hers.

It made no sense. Defied all reason and design.

No matter! She'd think later. For once, duty and joy melded. She held out her hand.

He grasped it. Striding the last two steps to the edge, he pulled her close as he planted one foot on the rim and stepped out, carrying her with him.

It was as if she'd flown for a few moments before he set her down and her feet rested on paved rock. They stood a mere arm's length apart. She felt her breasts rise and fall with her frantic breathing. She'd barely wrought any magick, but his need was written on his face and proclaimed in his stalwart erection. It seemed the very air about them stirred with desire.

"Sweet Adriana," he murmured as he wrapped a drying cloth around her shoulders. "You offer more than I have ever dreamed possible—beauty beyond compare and the generosity of an angel."

"You are my guest, Mark of Windhaw."

"Lady, nowhere in the realm would I find such hospitality."

Her heart snagged at the truth of that. "I fear," he said, as his hands patted her breasts through the drying cloth, "that I presume too much."

It was too late for hesitation, but as she looked up at his face, she read worry in his eyes. "What concerns you, Mark of Windhaw?"

"You, sweet Adriana." The back of his hand traced the outline of her cheek. "I fear I take advantage of your generosity. You are a woman here alone, and I know not when I can pass this way again."

Dear Rache! An Astrian with a conscience! "But you are here now, Mark of Windhaw, and now is the time we have." She closed her fingers round his wrist and lifted his hand to her mouth, kissing his knuckles before gently sucking his fingertips. "Our joining will be a sacred offering to Rache, here, by her consecrated springs."

"Sweet Adriana! Your ways here are so different from ours."

Indeed they were! "If you find me uncomely..." Slight chance indeed! His body was ripe with need and his eyes dark with desire.

"Dear heaven! No!"

Enough debate! "Let us offer ourselves to Rache." She pulled the drying linen off her shoulders and dropped it to the ground.

He needed no further persuading. As if throwing off the last of his restraints, he pulled her close and fastened his lips on hers. She let out a little yelp of need, surprise and delight as she opened her mouth to his. She responded with a heat that shocked her. Her mind was fogged by his strength and presence, the wild ardor of his kisses, and the heat of his still-damp body. His strong hands stroked her back and cupped her bottom. His cock was pressed tight and hard against her belly as she molded herself against him. As if she needed any confirmation of his desire!

She could not hold back the smile—or the sigh—as his lips kissed down her neck. Mark of Windhaw had a touch like no other man. Never had she known the wild thrills of pleasure that spiraled through her mind and possessed her body.

He paused for breath and murmured, "Sweet lady, you are truly a gift from the Gods!"

Time to offer a gift from the Five Goddesses!

Drawing back a little, she ran her hands over his chest and the still-damp mat of hair, dipping her head to suck each nipple until it stood hard and proud. His groan sang in her ears as she knelt, her hands resting on his strong thighs.

"Dear lady," he said, "why do you kneel to me, it is not..."

His voice choked off as she took his cock in her mouth. He was as surely muffled as she was. Pleasure took his tongue as hers gave. His hands grasped her head, caressing her hair as he moaned with need and pleasure. She sucked on the smooth, round head of his cock and slowly drew him deep into her mouth. A louder groan echoed in her ears, his thighs trembled under her hands as her lips worked up and down on the stem of his cock. He was smooth and hard, and tasted of man and the sacred freshness of Rache's consecrated spring. She felt his need as her tongue lapped up and down his hard flesh before circling the ridge below the head of his cock.

As she drew her mouth back, she flicked her tongue over the sweet, warm head of his cock, tasting male nectar. Yes,

Mark of Windhaw was ready. She drew back her mouth, resting on her heels as she looked up at him, his chest rising and falling with need, his eyes dark blue pools of desire, and his cock, if humanly possible, standing harder and prouder than ever.

Her own heart raced at the prospect of his cock seated deep inside her. Why this sweet ache between her legs? And this wild yearning to feel his male force within her body? What matter? If need and duty met then obligation became sweet pleasure, and the sight of Mark of Windhaw, aroused male, was pleasure indeed.

She circled his cock with her fingers and stroked it as she kissed first one ball, then the other. His moan was loud enough to echo off the stone walls surrounding them.

"Enough, dear love." He pulled away, grasping her hands in his fists. "I would not spill before I give you equal pleasure." He drew her to her feet and led her the short distance to the furs spread on the ground. "Now," he said, a smile of anticipation curling his mouth, "it is my turn to offer homage."

Gently he laid her on her back, tucking the furs under her head, insisting she be comfortable—as if it truly mattered to him. He sat beside her, his eyes caressing her body, his fingers tracing the outline of her breasts and the curve of her hip. His lips brushed her arms and belly and the soft inside of her wrist. It seemed his eager lips covered every inch of her from the rounded flesh of her shoulders, to the smooth skin behind her knees and at the base of her neck. He even kissed each toe, then ran his lips up the side of her leg while she lay back and let the novel but wondrous sensations flood her mind.

Never had her duty to Rache entailed this joy. Never had she dreamed of such delight, and from an Astrian! Sweet Rache, was he the one using magick? Impossible! They scorned the

Goddesses' ways. But how could an unbeliever offer such bliss? What matter—it served Rache's purpose.

He paused in his kisses, but only to caress her cunt. Cool air touched her inner flesh as he parted her nether lips. His breath came warm on her tender flesh, one moment before his mouth came down—there—and her brain flashed out. Thought was impossible as her senses drowned in rapture.

He breathed on her flesh to cool her before heating her anew with his lips. His tongue lapped her until she yearned for more and then he kissed with lips soft as thistle down. His beard brushed with a gentle abrasion as his kisses soothed and stirred all at once. When she thought he could offer no greater joy, need built like a strange fire between her legs. He narrowed his tongue and mouth onto her very point of ache and sent her bucking with need. It was as if her entire mind, heart and being were centered on one core of flesh. What was this man that he could do this? He brought such wildness and joy with nothing but his lips.

He latched onto that nub as if drawing life from her, but he was not taking, he was giving. His lips and tongue drove wild need and sweet desire to an intensity that all but scrambled thought. She was only half-aware of her little mewls of pleasure as the sweet ache grew and flooded her reason. It was as if she were taking flight. Her body tensed, rocking in a strange yet wondrous rhythm as he kept pace with her need.

She wanted to lie here forever, to never move from this spot, to accept his adoration for the rest of her days—to feel this joy, this wildness to enslave him to her. But higher and wilder her body stirred. Her mewls became grunts of delight and cries of joy. Pleasure built on sensation until, with a great flaring of passion, she screamed aloud, shouting Mark's name to the heavens. She was lost in a maelstrom of emotion. Flying on the joy in every muscle and sinew, she collapsed, a shaking trembling heap, as he wrapped his arms around her and held her close until the wild raging of her body calmed.

"Sweet lady," he whispered into her hair. "You are truly magnificent in your ecstasy."

She opened her eyes. The world still spun around her, but his arms anchored her to reality. "What magick have you wrought?" For truly it had to be magick. Her body still drifted as if on an ocean of pleasure.

"No magick, lady. Just the enchantment of our bodies and the power of our desire."

Heady power indeed! It was scarce believable! But neither could she deny the wild sensations his mouth created...or her body's amazing response. "Must be Astrian magick, Mark of Windhaw, for never in all my days have I dreamed of such power and pleasure. Is it possible ever to replicate such joy?"

"Very possible, lady. As yet we are not done."

Yes. Her body stiffened a little. To draw him in her power, he must enter her with his cock. It seemed a travesty to end this wonder with carnal rutting, but needs must... "Sir, I am yours." And soon he would be Rache's.

Chapter Four

It was with tenderness that he settled between her legs, his mouth fluttering kisses over her belly until the same strange yearning reawakened deep in her center. She shifted closer. He grasped her hips, lifting them a little, and entered her gently and easily, like water flowing over smooth rocks. As he came deep, she let out a slow sigh of utter pleasure. Minutes earlier, she'd thought it impossible to feel more pleasure. How wrong she'd been! This was far beyond the earlier joy. Slowly, he stroked within her—a wondrous rhythm of carnal delight. Little sighs and cries accompanied his groans of pleasure as he took her upon another whirlwind of sensation. Faster and harder he moved, her body echoing his. Her hips rocked to the same tempo. It seemed they breathed in unison. Even their hearts beat to the same pulse. She lifted her hips higher still, arching to meet his thrusts. He stiffened as he cried out her name. With a series of wild strokes, he came, pouring his strength into her. And as the first warmth reached her core, her body responded, leaping in yet another paroxysm of pleasure that left her once again weak, shaking and sweating with joy.

He loomed over her, taking his weight on his strong arms as he bent low and kissed her. "Sweet Adriana," he said, "you are the Lady Wonder of the warm springs. A haven for a lost traveler and a shelter for wanderers."

He eased his cock out of her, and she felt the loss as never before. Stretched alongside her, he smiled, his eyelids heavy with satiation and his face flushed with satisfaction. "Dear lady, we are now bound. A sharing such as ours comes seldom in a lifetime. I would I could stay here in the forest with you, but duty calls."

And duty called her! Never before had she hesitated. "What was it that happened between us?"

"Magick."

"Astrian magick?" If so, he was the first with this power.

"Let us call it the magick of Adriana of the springs, and Mark, the emperor's auditor."

Mention of the emperor brought her back to her task at hand. She must not lie here under the blue sky and lose herself in Mark's body and his wondrous kisses. But neither could she take his mind as she had her other victims. But how could she not? She had her sacred oath.

"Sweet Adriana, what disturbs your peace? A shadow of worry passed behind your eyes."

And over her heart. But... "We both have our appointed roles, Mark of Windhaw. You have the emperor's commission and I have my duties to my Goddess. Both must intrude in this glorious now."

He sighed. "Aye. I must go." His voice sounded heavy, as if laden with unhappiness. "I must find my page. He's but a lad and I sent him on a man's mission. I hope to meet him in Merridale." He turned to her, his eyes bright with tears. "It breaks my heart to leave you, sweetling. But I will return... You have the word of Mark of Windhaw. I cannot say when. I must fulfill my oath to my emperor. There are people whose lives and futures depend on me."

"What will you do in Merridale?" Besides this university of the emperor's.

"I must take reckoning of injustices and claims." He sighed. "It will not be an easy task. There are those who would lie and conceal the truth."

"What might they conceal?"

"Adriana, deep in these woods, you are protected from the hazards and calamities of the world." Little did he know. "During the wars, many ills were wrought. Some appointed officers abused their authority. Word came back slowly to the capital and now the emperor has sent parties to establish the truth."

It was hard to believe, but why would he lie? "And if it is found ills were done?"

"The guilty will be called to account."

"Perhaps..."

He looked offended at that. "You question my word, lady?"

"Not your word." That was true enough. "But can the truth be discovered after all these years?"

"Why not? Memories are long when hurt occurs."

Very true. Could she truly believe him? But if this were true, she needed him auditing in Merridale, not wandering naked and lost in the forest. What to do? "Will you just go to Merridale, sir?"

"I will go wherever needed in this quadrant. Once I have my page and a fresh horse, I can hire another recorder."

How far could she trust him? Her heart wanted to accept his word and beg for justice for her people, but her head insisted she owed him to Rache. "Have you heard of Endholm, Mark of Windhaw?"

"No, lady, should I have?"

Now to pick her words with care. "There was talk, some years back, of slain villagers and burned cottages."

His eyes went almost black with anger. "You are sure? What did you hear?"

"That after the attack none were left alive."

"What about children? The women?"

She shook her head. After all these years, the remembered horror tightened her throat and tears stung behind her eyelids.

"It shall be investigated. You have my word. If wrong was done, those responsible will answer before the emperor."

What now? Mark of Windhaw had to ride away. But she dared not let him go with knowledge of her sanctuary. She should follow her course, take his mind and abandon him in the woods. But then the debt for her family's death—and who knew how many others—would go uncollected. Mark of Windhaw had the power to call the guilty to account.

"Sweet Adriana." He kissed her cheek. "With a heavy heart, I must leave you, but you have my word I will return."

That could never be. What now? She had to let him go...but ensure he never returned. With the others, she'd taken all memories but of her so that they wandered lost and fevered, ever searching for what they'd never find. Why not reverse the power? Take from him all memory of her, so he could then ride on and dispense justice, but never return. Her heart skipped a beat at that, but it was her only choice. It would deliver justice and leave Mark a whole man.

This called for a change in plans. "For the joy you have given me, let me prepare a last refreshment."

"Ever gracious, sweet Adriana."

Ever torn! "'Tis little enough, Mark of Windhaw, for what we shared." She sensed he was tempted to tarry, as much as her body yearned for more caresses. It was late, but she could use that to her advantage. "Let me brew you an infusion to help throw off fatigue as you ride." As she spoke, she rested her hand on his forehead and willed sleep on him.

She lay beside him longer than she should have, but lingering was so bittersweet. Never before had she faced this quandary. The others who had come had taken her with the coarseness and haste she'd expected. It had been no stretch to see them as the wreakers of havoc. She had had no hesitation leaving them to wander, unable to injure another female.

Had ever another priestess faced this dilemma? Should she put her oath and mission ahead of her wish for retribution? Was not that same retribution her sworn task?

Mark had to leave her a whole man, with mind enough to exercise his commission and the emperor's desire for justice. But he could not go with knowledge of her haven.

But...if he left with no memory of her and his time in the shrine...? It would be as if he'd never wandered her way in the mist. But she would always know the Astrian who'd treated her with honor and respect and sought justice for the oppressed.

Mind made up, she pulled on her shift and gown and tightened her girdle, pausing only to cover Mark with a spare fur. She returned to her cave, then climbed the escarpment above the cool spring. Mark of Windhaw's mount responded to her call. How could she resist her magick? She'd honed her skills under fine mentors. Eadyyl and Eadwyn had loved her as mothers. How would they look upon her decision? Was it the right one? No time to even pray for guidance. Mark's horse approached. Time to ready his departure.

Back down on the ground, Adriana gathered herbs from her stores and hot water from the source and left the herbs to steep.

She carried the saddlebags and his cloak out into the sunshine. With the halter in hand, she awaited the horse's approach. The beast was none too happy to accept the bit after her freedom, but she must face her duty as Adriana must now face hers.

Mark's saddle and leathers she set on a rock by the stream while she walked around the beast, weaving a spell of surefootedness. She dreaded Mark falling injured as his companion had, as the way from here to Merridale was rough in places. Mount protected, she left the animal to graze on the soft turf while she set another spell of protection about Mark's cloak.

Satisfied she had done all she could to ease his travel, she now had to set her mind and skills to the potion of endurance. It was strong and golden colored like the autumn crocuses. She had made a good quantity, enough to fill two drinking cups. To work the time delay spell on his memory, she would need all the strength she could muster.

Setting the cups to one side, she burned sacred herbs before her doorway and prayed for strength and power. As the small flame died, she took the cooling ash and sprinkled it along the path that led away from her haven.

The horse chomped by the side of the stream, and Adriana paused to run her hands down the animal's neck. A fine and handsome beast—a deep brown like ripe nuts after a hard frost, with a mane as black as the darkest corner of a cave. The beast whinnied at her touch as if sensing the power in her hands. Mark of Windhaw might doubt wood magick, but his mount knew better.

Leaving the horse by the cool spring, Adriana reentered her cave, took the two cups from the ledge and carried them through the tunnel to where Mark still slumbered. Naked.

Indeed, he was comely in his skin and since this was the last time she would ever see him, she would indulge her yearning and feast her eyes, stealing one final sight of his glorious male beauty.

Setting the cups down on the edge of the warm pool, she knelt beside him and brushed his fair hair from his face. How strange life was! That this man of honor and gentleness was of the same stock as the oppressors. Mayhap there were others of his ilk. It was that hope that justified her sparing him. If Mark of Windhaw and others of the emperor's appointment could set things right then she would speed him on his way with all the aid she could summon.

Stifling a sigh at her coming loss, she kissed his cheek, brushing her lips across the rasp of his beard. She wanted to bottle the sensation of her lips on his skin and the scent of sleeping male. Preserve it to remember during the future without him. He'd promised to return. She had to ensure he never would.

"Dear sir," she whispered, smoothing his hair off his face. "My love." She almost choked on the words she never thought to utter. "Mark of Windhaw, the night has passed and you must awaken."

At her word, his eyes flashed open, dark pools of clear blue looked up at her as he smiled and reached out. She let him pull her head down and permitted herself the indulgence of a kiss. The sweetness of his touch brought tears to the corners of her eyes. She could not, would not, weaken.

"I hate to leave you, dear Adriana," he said, "and you have my word I will return. I will mark with flashes the path back to your dwelling."

More work to conceal the tracks, but necessary. "I have brought an infusion of herbs. It will give you strength and alertness on your way. I also have a pouch of such herbs. If you tire on the road, just steep them in hot water to restore you energies."

"You are too kind, Lady Adriana." He looked up at the sun climbing overhead. "Alas, I must go. I never meant to tarry this long, but I bless the Five Gods that I lost my way and found you."

So saying he stood, and once again, she feasted her eyes on the sheer male beauty of this man. This Astrian. Her lover. This soul of honor who would avenge the slain and dispossessed. She stood as he walked over to his clothes she'd folded neatly. She watched as he pulled on his leather breeks and tunic, marveling at the turn of his thigh, the curve of his knees and the flat plane of his belly. She handed him his belt as she straightened his tunic. He kissed her fingertips as he took it. It took all her strength to stifle the sigh.

Dressed, he took both cups and handed her one before sitting beside her. They were not touching. It was as if he, too, was aware of closeness that would test both their resolves.

"Your health, sweet Adriana," he said, raising his cup.

"And yours, Mark of Windhaw. May your mission prosper."

"Aye." He shook his head and smiled at her. "Duty is a hard mistress. Would I could stay here with you, but to do so I would be forsworn."

"Then you must go. Honor is of great worth to both of us."

He sipped again, licking the sweet brew from his lips. "'Tis a strange infusion, lady."

"A blend of forest herbs. Together, they banish fatigue. Now you will ride without tiring and arrive refreshed. Do not take it too often, and never more than two days at a stretch, but you have a supply if needed."

They sat in silence for several minutes, watching the sun dance on the still waters. A blue pelwit flying low to peck at moss on a rock was the only other sign of life. It was as if time hesitated. For these few fleeting minutes, they had each other, before the world reclaimed him.

Knowing tears were close, she stood. "Dear sir. I would keep you here forever if I could, but..."

"Aye." He rose. "I must away. How the tales of evil lurking in these woods lied. Here, in the deep forest, I found beauty beyond compare." She took his hand and together they walked around the rim of the pool toward the tunnel. He paused and looked over his shoulder before entering as if to imprint on his mind the memory of their time beside the water. A memory she had to erase.

Adriana paused in the cave to fill a small bag with the promised herbs. If they could help him later, so be it. Rache could spare a few dried leaves.

When she reached him, he was saddling his mount. Soon, too soon, he would be gone forever. The horse whinnied and stamped her hooves in her need to be away.

Mark of Windhaw paused after tightening the girths and took a step toward Adriana. "Nothing I can say can measure what burns inside me. Sweet Adriana, I will, I must return. For surely we are soulmates. Wait for me. It may be weeks before my work is done, but I will come. You have my word."

"Speak not of the future. Let me remember a constant now." Standing on tiptoe, she cupped his face with her hands, her fingertips brushing his cheeks and forehead. As his lips came down, she blocked out the sensations, forcing her mind on his, willing him to forget her and this place. Forcing forgetfulness into his heart and will. What more could she do? "Let me have a token," she asked. "A kerchief."

He pulled one from his pocket. "'Tis scarce enough, Adriana." It was enough to weave the spell. "Wait!" He pulled a heavy gold ring off his finger. "Take this, my love. It is the seal of my house. This is my pledge that I will return."

Her fingers closed over the metal. Warm from his skin.

"I will guard it," she said, "and remember." For the rest of her days.

With a last kiss, he mounted and turned down the hill. At the curve, he looked back and waved. Adriana watched as he disappeared through the trees. She would never see him again.

She blinked back the tears that pricked behind her eyelids. No time now for pity. With his handkerchief, she could work stronger magick still. She lit a small fire, brought out a small flagon of oil and more herbs and spread the handkerchief on the rocks. As the herbs burned, she sang a hymn to Rache—a long song of supplication. Her own loss was her offering to Rache. Offered in return for the safety of Mark of Windhaw who had come to right old wrongs. Adriana built the ceremonial fire higher, casting on handfuls of dried hayweed and forra root. All day, she tended the fire, her mind seeing Mark as he rode out of the forest across farmland. As the sun dipped, she cast his handkerchief on the fire. It flared and burned fast, and as the ash cooled she gathered it up and cast it into the water. She watched the last gray traces float down the stream. He was gone from her life and, as soon as the sun set, he would remember her no more.

Taking advantage of the last of the daylight, she set out down the path to check the trail. True to his word, he'd set blazes on the trees and marked a dividing of the way with rocks. No matter. Rocks were reset and marked bark muddied or disguised. She planted a fast growing climber against one blaze and on another she cut off the limb. Returning along the path, she brushed the way behind her with a leafy branch.

The path was hidden. No traveler would ever find the shrine unless she called him. And she would not call. Not while she carried Mark of Windhaw in her heart.

She made it up the last few turns until she saw the flat rocks where she and Mark had shared their food. Misery swept over her. She ran the last few paces and threw herself on her sleeping furs. The lingering male scent of her lover undid her utterly. She buried her head in the furs and let her tears fall free, lamenting her loss. By the time the moon rose over the escarpment, she had cried herself to sleep.

ལ ♡

Adriana slept fitfully and woke with an aching head and eyes sore from weeping. She, who'd always slept alone, yearned to feel Mark's body beside her. Lying awake at dawn, she fancied she heard Mark's horse whinny outside; she even ran to see, but there was no horse, phantom or otherwise, only the stream burbling down the hill and birds welcoming the sunrise. For one bereft moment, she regretted erasing all traces of the horse's hoofs.

She was demented! Mark of Windhaw was gone. And forever! She remained. She still had her calling to protect the sacred springs and serve her Goddess. For a few heart-wrenching minutes, she looked down the path to the bend where she'd last seen Mark of Windhaw as he waved farewell. Enough! She must bury her loss in service and labor. She would spend the day gathering herbs and berries. That resolved, she strode up the path and climbed to the top of the escarpment to watch the sun rise over the trees. As the glory of another golden morning warmed the air, she called Hareth, her largest goat. Whatever she gathered, Hareth could carry with ease.

Descending to the ground, she entered her cave to gather bags and baskets, but hesitated at the glint of shining metal on the path. A silver button from Mark's tunic! Wisdom dictated she destroy it—throw it in the stream or bury it deep. Foolishness brought more comfort. While Hareth arrived and chewed on the daisies by the stream, Adriana took a steel trade needle and sewed the button inside the pocket of her cloak. No one would ever see it, but she could finger the raised crest of the metal—if she ever wished. Now she had two mementos of her love—the ring, even now heavy on a thread around her neck, and the button hidden in her pocket. No one would ever see them, but she would always know.

She strapped leather bags and a pair of baskets on Hareth's back, packed dried berries and roots and filled two water skins. Cloak over her shoulders and walking staff in hand, she set off deep into the forest.

CR ℘

She had a linen-lined basket half-full of sweetberries and several pouches of herbs by the time she paused for rest. Roots did not taste the same without ham. Best forget that! Roast roots and berries had satisfied her before. They would now. She stood up, brushed the grass and dust off her skirts and took hold of Hareth's leash. She had many more hours of light and a good way ahead there was a grove of purple drupe trees. It was too early to pick them, but if the crop looked to be as heavy as last year, she would bring extra baskets to gather them later. Best be prepared.

She had walked for a distance, skirting a shallow trench overgrown with brambles and wild vines. She was near the edge of the forest and walked cautiously, alert to sounds of intruders or travelers passing the forest fringes, when she heard a noise. Not a horse or even a foot traveler, it sounded like the mewl of a weak puppy—a sound she'd not heard since childhood. Memories tumbled back of playing with the litter of puppies with her sisters...and fast on that pleasant memory came images of the slaughter. Enough! Mark would right that wrong. But the sound continued. Whatever creature lurked in the undergrowth, it was too weak to do harm.

Leaving Hareth nibbling a bush, Adriana drew her skirts tight and gingerly parted the vines and brambles with her staff. The sound came from her left. The deeper she walked in the trench, the louder and clearer the cries.

"Never mind, puppy, I'm coming."

A louder mewl answered her, and then a weak distorted human voice. "Help. I beg you!"

Shocked, she ran the last few meters, heedless of the scratches on her legs and arms. In a hollow lay the naked body of a child. A boy, she realized, as she came closer. An injured boy. His feet and legs were bleeding, and his body was covered with scratches. A trail of broken and bent bracken lay behind him. He must have crawled this far along the base of the ditch, but had been too weak to climb out. Yet he was not too feeble to look up and beg.

"Lady, I entreat you." He held up his arm, and Adriana stared in horror at his bloodied swollen fingers, and his face, bruised and swollen, eyes half-closed.

Who could have done this? Astrians! Who else? Bile rose to her throat at the realization that this child had perhaps been battered by the man she'd shared her bed with yesterday. The man she'd let ride away unharmed! Ye Goddesses, how had she been duped!

Time later to dwell on that mistake! Now she had a child to tend. "I can help you," she told him, pulling off her cloak and covering him. "It will take time, and will pain you when I move you."

"Lady," he mumbled through his swollen face. "Take me anywhere, I fear they may return."

"I will protect you." Mist could hide as well as distract and in this hollow they could bide if need be. Listening, she heard no others nearby. Whoever his attackers were, they had long gone. They were safe enough but it would be no easy task to lift him out. "Wait," she said. "I will be back."

She went up the slope to fetch a waterleather, the linen liner from one of the baskets and a pouch of herbs. She could ease his immediate pain and cleanse his wounds, but how to get him out? The boy could not walk on his injured feet. He might be able, with her help, to crawl up the sides of the trench, but he couldn't drag himself the several hours needed to return to her cave. And he was far too heavy to carry. A travois might serve.

She climbed back down; the child opened his eyes at her approach. "Lady, I have been so afraid..."

She understood fear of the Astrians. "Hush, you will be safe. Here, drink." She held the water skin and he gulped down mouthfuls. Who knew how long he'd been lying here? "I can bind up your wounds and clean them a little, but to treat them properly I must take you to my home where I have herbs and salves."

"I cannot walk, lady."

"No matter, I can construct a travois to carry you to my home. It will take me a little time, and first, I must dress your wounds." She handed him a sliver of andine bark from her bag. "Suck on this. It will ease your pain."

It also left him drowsy, but all the better. Using a torn scrap of linen, she washed off his wounds. It took all her control not to gasp in horror. The soles of his feet had been burned with hot irons, and the bleeding swollen fingers had had nails ripped out. Who could be so inhuman?

Astrians! And she'd permitted one to seduce her from her path with gibber about learning and justice while his cohorts tortured a child and left him naked in the forest for the wild animals to finish off.

But she would foil them. Utterly.

She had to get the boy to safety at the shrine and the day was passing. Building a travois to carry him would take time. She had to cut the branches she needed and getting him up the slope would be a painful labor—for both of them.

Best start now.

Chapter Five

The sun had dropped halfway to setting by the time she'd hacked enough branches and lashed them together. Hareth was willing to be led down the slope, but was less than pleased to have the weight of the travois harnessed to his back. It was unfortunate, but necessary. She could never have moved the child on her own. He cried out in pain as she dragged him to the travois, but she placed more bark in his mouth. Then, steeling herself to ignore his cries, she strapped him to the branches with her belt and lengths of young vines.

At her urging, Hareth complied and hauled the injured boy up and out of the trench. As they set homeward, Hareth picked up the pace just a little. Along the way, the child fainted. Perhaps it was a mercy.

They reached the shrine as the sun was dipping on the horizon. Adriana led Hareth inside, unfastened the strapping and lowered the travois to the ground. "You're safe now," she told the child. "I must tend your injuries properly, but will first brew you a draught to ease the pain and help you rest."

Dark eyes looked up at her from his ashen face. "Lady, they mean ill to my lord."

"I know," she replied, touching the small hand clutching her cloak that still covered him. "They do harm wherever they go. But they can never find you here." He relaxed a little, but pain still etched his face. "I have salve and potions to help heal your hurts."

He drank the infusion willingly, but when she started to bathe him with warm water, his nudity shamed him. She saw that from his averted eyes and his attempts to turn away. But if she did not cleanse the wounds, they would fester. He had injuries enough without adding infection to his ills. So as she bathed him, she talked to him. She told him he was now safe under the Goddess Rache's protection and none could hurt him. How she herself had been rescued from harm and had learned the way of the forest.

Was it an omen, she wondered, that she would find an injured boy, just as she'd been found and rescued? Time would tell. She sensed deep in her heart it was more than chance that she had found him—that their futures were linked.

But for now, his future lay in rest. He was all but asleep by the time she dressed his last wounds. She propped his shoulders on a rolled-up cover and fetched the infusion of andine bark with poppy seed to help him sleep. "Drink," she said. "It will ease the pain and help you sleep."

He nodded and sipped as she held the bowl. When he had finished, she lowered his head and covered him with sleeping furs. He was asleep in minutes.

She lit a small fire to keep the child warm and stepped out by the stream and wove a spell of protection around them. The effort drained her after the day's exertions and she, too, was asleep at once.

CR ED

She woke to dawn light gleaming through the cave opening. The child was, as she'd hoped, still deep in drugged sleep, and if she'd measured aright, would sleep the day around. The longer the better. Rest would heal him and she needed to fashion crutches for when he was well enough to move. His right foot was hideously burned and would take weeks to heal. But for now, she must needs take care of herself. She'd fallen asleep without washing and still had leaves and twigs in her hair from the forest. One look at her arms and legs showed she had scratches that needed care.

She went straight to the bathing pool, forcing her mind not to dwell on her time there with Mark of Windhaw. That had been a weakness she would never repeat. The shame of being so easily duped would gnaw her soul if permitted. She did not have time to dwell on her foolishness or his perfidy; she had an injured child to heal. Clean and refreshed, she climbed out and dried herself quickly, pulling on a clean shift and her brushed-down gown.

As she bent to gather the damp drying cloths and her old shift, she noticed a crumpled pile of white linen—Mark of Windhaw's forgotten shirt. Much as it would have satisfied her soul to cast the garment on her fire, she decided, no. The shirt would serve as cover for the lad's nakedness. Clothing him would be a difficulty. Eadwyn and Eadyyl had cut down their shifts and gowns to fit her as a child, but a boy needed breeches. The shirt was a start. If only she'd stolen, as she had first planned, from Mark of Windhaw's packs.

Too late for that! Somehow she would fashion clothes for the child. And until he could move with ease, the shirt would serve. She ate a hasty breakfast of fruit and a handful of last year's waynuts. The child slept on so she didn't venture far from the cave. She had yesterday's—admittedly small—harvest of herbs and roots and in the days ahead would need generous amounts of salve and potions.

She spent the day preparing infusions for when the child awoke. She climbed the far wall of the warm shrine to where her birds nested and found three brown eggs. These she set in the warm pool to cook for when the boy woke needing food. A convalescing child needed more than roots. Some of Mark's ham or cheese would be welcome. For the second time, she regretted not raiding his saddlebags. She did, though, leave the boy long enough to walk to where her goats grazed, returning with a bowl of warm milk.

By late afternoon, the child stirred and, with Adriana's help, hobbled out into the open to relieve himself. He barely woke and scarcely spoke before falling asleep again. As she covered him back with the furs, Adriana remembered the crutches Eadyyl had fashioned so she could walk those long years ago.

A tree, a short walk away furnished two forked branches. Adriana stripped away the bark as she sat watching the sunset. Gathering the shavings into a pile for tinder, she smoothed the wood and bound the wide fork at the top of each with strips of leather. The height she would gauge when the child woke.

Early the next morning, she changed his dressings. He barely stirred as she loosed the bandages, and Adriana was pleased to see the smallest wounds healing already. Must be the powers of Rache's water and the magick stirred into the healing potions. When the child woke completely, she would immerse him in the warm spring.

Astrians were animals! No, lower than animals! No beast of the forest used their young thus! Looking at the dark bruises on the child's face, Adriana took an oath to herself and Rache. No one would ever harm this boy again. He would stay here, deep in the forest, and never venture near the destroying Astrians.

She had thrived under Eadyyl and Eadwyn's care. So would he. He could learn the forest ways. Seldom had a boy studied magick, but was there any law or custom to prohibit it? She must ask her mentors. When the child's leg healed, they could travel to visit the shrine of Aenwath and consult the two priestesses who'd reared her.

CR SO

The boy woke refreshed and ravenous early the next morning. She gave him the crutches and he gladly hobbled out to relieve himself. Seeing how he was still shamed by his nudity, Adriana wrapped her cloak around him while he fed. He wolfed down the eggs, most of her store of roasted roots, two large cups of goat's milk and a pile of the berries she'd gathered before she found him.

Sated, he leaned back against the cave wall and asked, "Lady, who are you, and where am I?"

"I am Adriana, and this is my home. I found you injured and brought you here. Who are you?"

He hesitated, an uneasy frown between his wary eyes. "I am Pait. I thank you for your aid." There was a strange formality in his speech and a clear hesitation and uncertainty. That, she understood.

"Pait, those who tried to harm you will never find you here."

"But they would harm my lord...I must warn him."

"I think first, you must wash. I don't know how long you lay in the forest, but you have slept here nigh on two days. Once you are clean, I have a shirt you may wear. Other clothes, we must make shift. Keep my cloak around you and I will take you to the warm pool."

His wonder equaled Mark of Windhaw's. Pait stood open-mouthed as he wobbled on his crutches. "What is this place, lady?"

"A safe haven from the harm and hurt in the world." She led him to the warm cascade, gave him a drying cloth and Mark's discarded shirt—now folded smooth—and left Pait to his ablutions. "When you have washed, I will redress your wounds and shorten your crutches so you can move more easily. If you need me, call."

He took half the morning washing. She resisted the temptation to offer help and took the time to build up the fire and prepare more roots for roasting. Seeing Pait eat brought back memories of the quantities her brother had eaten. She would need to increase her stores, but for now, her roots and nuts would sustain them both for a day or two. She wanted to ask the boy who had mistreated him and why, but remembering her own horror for days after the assault on her village, she resolved to hold back. Give Pait time to heal, let him realize he was safe, and, once she had earned his trust, he would tell her.

It might take weeks, but she had time.

Roots set in the embers to roast, she went back into her store for some of last season's dried drupes. They were shriveled but still sweet, and Pait would like them.

CR SO

"Lady, where is my lord?" Pait cried out, as he hobbled toward her, the shirt covering him to his knees, dragging her cloak behind him.

"Pait," she began, "who is your lord, and why should I know where he is?"

The boy drew himself up as straight as he could on too-tall crutches. "I am sworn to Mark of Windhaw, and here is his token!" He pulled the cloak from behind him and tossed it at her. Overbalancing as one crutch shifted, he fell in a heap.

A token! Mark of Windhaw! The silver button she'd sewn into her cloak pocket, back when she was still enamored with her Astrian lover, but... She put her thoughts and questions on hold as she went to help Pait, who was using all his strength to sit upright. He accepted her help unwillingly.

"You have harmed him! You will suffer for that when the emperor hears!"

A brave child—was he unaware of his isolation and helplessness? "Pait, come and sit by the fire. Tell me about your lord, and why you believe he was here."

He reached for her cloak and, as she'd suspected, turned out the pocket and exposed the silver button. "That is my lord's token," Pait said. "He had it embossed on the buttons of his tunic. The oatlen tree is the sign of his house."

The same tree engraved on the gold ring that still hung around her neck. "Yes, Pait. He was here. Wrap the cloak around you and listen to me." Now, how much to tell? "Your lord, Mark of Windhaw, was here. He was lost in the mist. Three days ago. He stopped to rest, and we shared our food..." no need to dwell on what else they'd shared, "...and, after washing—that discarded shirt was his, left by accident—he went on his way."

Pait bit his lip, his eyes misty with worry. "Did he say, lady, where he was going?"

"To Merridale."

The child's eyes filled with tears and he shook his head. "Then I have, indeed, betrayed him!"

"Unlikely!"

He reached forward and grasped her sleeve. "Lady, you do not understand!"

That much was clear. "Make me understand, Pait."

He nodded, sniffed back his tears and wiped his eyes with the back of his hand. "Lady," he began, "this is what happened..."

Adriana listened with curiosity, interest and then mounting horror. "They tortured you, knowing you served Mark of Windhaw?"

"Lady, they tortured me because I served him. I did not understand, at first, why the commander took the sigil and refused to return it. Then he asked questions, more than seemed right, and when I refused to answer, he called the inquisitor. I knew then that whatever they asked, I must not tell. But when the pain began..." he paused to sniff and shudder, "...I would have told them anything to make them stop. And now I have betrayed my lord. They sent messengers ahead to the master of Merridale." He looked down at his injured feet and held up his injured hands, bleeding from grasping the crutches. "If they did this to me, what will they do to him?"

It was the tears trailing down the child's cheeks that almost undid Adriana. "Nothing if we can prevent it!"

His wide eyes and dropped jaw echoed the astonishment swirling in her mind. She was proposing aiding an Astrian—and at some considerable risk to herself. What did she think she could do against a company of soldiers? Whatever was possible!

"What can we do, lady? I'm crippled and you are a witch of the—" He broke off, coloring and looking everywhere but at her.

"I am a witch of the woods?" she finished. "Yes, I know what you Astrians call the priestesses of the Goddess. They think we are insane, old women gathering herbs. They err." As she spoke, she felt the power of Rache rise within her. She must not waste it on anger and her indignation. She must plan this. Carefully.

"Pait, first let me bind up your hands and feet again. Then let me think what we must do."

He sat quietly as she ripped up a spare shift for more bandages and dressed his wounds with salve. As she finished, she brewed an herb infusion for both of them, then helped him outside to sit in the last light of the failing afternoon.

"We must plan what to do to help your master." And her lover... "Tell me, Pait, when did they abandon you in the woods?"

He frowned, thinking back. "I remember lying there all afternoon and through the dark before you found me."

"And when did they leave Fort Antin?"

"That morning early. Quel told them to take me into the forest the evening before. But they left it until morning. I heard them muttering they would not venture into the woods near nightfall."

So it was three days since they had left him, and two since Mark had ridden away. But Astrians would travel around the forest... "Their cowardice gives us a little time and advantage, Pait. Are you afraid of traveling through the forest?"

He took a deep breath. "Not with you, lady."

He was a poor liar, but she could not but appreciate his courage. "They will not dare travel through it, of that I am certain. Did the party headed for Merridale leave the same time as the party that abandoned you in the forest?"

"They left ahead of us, lady."

Bad news. They could well be ahead of Mark of Windhaw, but perhaps she could overtake him and warn him. If not, they could at least reach Merridale. "We need to leave as soon as we can get ready. I know faster paths than the ways used by the soldiers."

"Lady," Pait looked at her, his face worried, "I can scarce walk."

"You can ride on Hareth." He looked as if stumbling on foot was preferable. "Not on a rough travois. You may ride. Not the best way to travel, but it will suffice." She paused. "Quel's men may arrive before us. We must avoid them. There is little likelihood they will be watching for you, but even so, someone may recognize you. We will hide you."

"Lady, if my lord is in danger, I will not hide."

"You will hide in plain sight, Pait. Listen. I travel to Merridale once or twice a year to barter herbs and potions for trade goods. I will make an extra trip this year." She smiled at him. "No one will remark if I have an assistant. When I was a child, I traveled there with my mentors."

"Lady, I have only this shirt! I cannot go like this!"

She smiled at his outraged sense of modesty. "We can manage better. I will cut down an old gown and tuck up that cloak. You must go as a girl, I'm afraid. We have no time to alter a gown into breeches, and if they are by any chance watching for you, they will not be looking for a girl."

His face showed what he thought of that plan, but he made no more objections. "When will we leave, lady?"

"As soon as I can get ready. There is a strong moon tonight so the dark will not hamper us. If we go straight through the forest—a way those traitorous soldiers would not dare—we can be in Merridale by midday." What they would do when they reached Merridale, she had no idea. She could scarcely stand in the market place and call for Mark of Windhaw, but she had hours ahead to plan that step.

Once they got going.

CR SO

It took less time than she'd anticipated. Pait helped, hobbling on his crutch to fill waterleathers, and fitting packets of herbs, pots of salve and vials of potions into packs. Adriana gathered together most of her food in case of delays, or if they needed to hide. She would not share her anxieties with Pait, but if they did find Mark, what could three of them do against a traitorous garrison?

Enough forward worries! She must concentrate on her first task, getting herself and Pait to Merridale ahead of Quel's men—if possible. While Pait packed dried fruit and cheese in the last bag, she hacked off the bottom of her old cloak and tacked up the hem. Then she set to fashioning a skirt of the trimmings. Mark's old shirt would serve as a shift and petticoat, and she had an old shawl that she used during winter. Pait could wear that on top.

He was none too impressed at his clothing, but he thanked her politely and acquiesced willingly to her suggestion that they bind up his foot even more. "If they think you have a club foot or a deformity, they will look at you even less closely," she said.

He nodded, knowing the Astrians' ways even better than Adriana.

CR SO

Before leaving the shrine, Adriana called up the water and wove a mist. If the Astrians overcame their fear of the forest, she did not want them desecrating the sacred ground. Pait watched, his eyes wide with wonder—or was it fear?—as the mist rose at her bidding.

"Lady," he whispered, his voice tight with awe. "Is it devil magick you work?"

"Magick, yes, but magick of power and protection." Her heart cramped a little, remembering the victims she'd lured with her mist. "I am a priestess of the waters—I have learned how to raise mists." And used that power to avenge her murdered family. Enough! This was not the time to dwell on that or the years between. Pait had confirmed her instincts about Mark of Windhaw. She had spared him enchantment, but let him ride into danger from those he trusted. He would, mayhap, have been safer wandering the forest!

As they set off through the dark trees in the moonlight, she wondered briefly about her other victims. Had they too been honorable? No, they had taken her harshly, seeing her as a creature to be used, the feeling being mutual—until Mark of Windhaw. Before Mark, it had been nearly three years since she'd trapped the last Astrian. Did Mark, mayhap, mark a new Astrian? She shook her head. If the new Astrians were the ones who'd abused Pait, the new were no better than the old! But as she trod softly through the woods, she thought about Mark's mission. If there were others who believed what Mark did, others sent out by the emperor to impose justice and establish foundations of learning, maybe a new world without hate and repression might dawn. Small wonder there were those who'd stop Mark! And they would succeed if she did not find him first.

She steered Hareth by pulling on the halter. Pait, perched atop the laden goat, smiled at her. How he trusted her! That too was an added worry. What if she never found Mark of Windhaw? What if he'd been waylaid on the road?

She could smother her soul with what-ifs! She must succeed. Find Mark of Windhaw. Warn him of the treachery, and then... She took a deep breath. She would hand Pait into his care and return to her home in the forest. All seemed satisfactory but the last. Impossible! She had her sworn oath. She must return. She had no choice.

She set her mind to the problem of how to find Mark of Windhaw in the teeming streets of Merridale. She had friends...well, not friends, but she had people she knew. The hostler where she stabled her goat, and Host Martten who ran the Demented Hare and always rented her an attic room at a fair price. He knew most of the gossip in the town. She would ask him about newcomers, or envoys from the emperor.

That decided, she settled into a steady rhythmic march. The moon was past its zenith. She had perhaps three more hours before dawn, and the peace and quiet of the forest seemed to be soothing rather than frightening Pait. He was half-dozing against the packs on Hareth's back.

Yes, it was a fine Goddess-given night, and the way was clear and firm underfoot. Perfect.

It was fifteen or twenty minutes further on that she first noticed the smell of smoke.

Chapter Six

Not a forest fire. It was too low and too little—unless just started. But who would be lighting night fires in the forest—or on the fringes? They were just a few hundred paces from where the Merri ran along the rim of the forest before heading toward Merridale. Adriana shook her head. She had not planned on encountering anyone until she neared the town, but arriving with other travelers might make their arrival less conspicuous.

Entering Merridale aside, she needed to know who lingered on the forest fringes. If the Astrians were overcoming their fear of the woods, it could only spell worry. She still saw them as enemy even as she went to rescue one. Life had its twists.

Pait woke as she stopped and anchored Hareth to a sapling. "Lady, is something amiss?"

She shook her head. "I think not, but there are people close. I must go and see."

Even in the half-light of moonlight, she saw Pait tense. "What if it is Quel's men?"

"We avoid them! I know the forest far better than they do." He seemed satisfied with her reply. "You stay here. Make sure Hareth does not eat himself free of his tether and wait until I return."

Watching the light flickering through the trees, she moved cautiously, easing through the shadows until she stood close enough to see. There were just three of them—two asleep, wrapped in their cloaks, and a third watching. Close by, their horses waited. As she watched, the seated one stood up and put more fuel on the fire. He was only a lad! Two men and a boy, equipped with horses and traveling cross-country. Merchants usually traveled in caravans and soldiers in troops, but she remembered Mark's words about other audit parties. Could this be one? If so, why were they here? Weren't they all working different quadrants? Were they soldiers?

She was tempted to wait until light when she could see more clearly, but she didn't have time to delay. Unfortunately, if she drew closer, she would risk being seen. She retraced her steps to Pait. "I need your help and your young eyes. There is a party camped nearby. Can you tell from a distance if they are soldiers?"

"I can try, lady."

Hareth made more noise than she did alone, but Pait's crutches would be useless on the soft ground, and she could hardly ask him to crawl. She stopped as close as she dared, but not as near as before, and Pait leaned forward from his perch, peering into the dark, his face intent on the shadowy figures by the fire. As they watched, one of the sleeping figures stirred, sat up and stood. He shook out his cloak and threw it over his shoulders. The lad seated by the fire turned and the taller figure said, "I'll take the watch, Allat. Get what sleep you can before…"

"Allat!" Pait's cry carried in the still of the night.

Horrified, Adriana reached out for Hareth's halter to pull him and Pait back into the safety of the forest, but the goat moved faster. Scared, perhaps, by the cry so close to his ear, he charged forward through the last of the trees and into the open, Pait clinging onto his back and crying out in terror.

Both men were awake and drawing swords.

"Pait!" Adriana raced after him. Hareth, seemingly intent on creating as much mayhem as one goat could contrive, raced toward the group, then veered sharply to the right. As he turned, Pait fell off with a cry. Adriana let Hareth go. He would return soon enough or at least head home, but Pait...

She rushed forward to be stopped by a tall dark-garbed man with a drawn sword.

"Lady, why go you here?"

"Would you stop me aiding my companion?"

"Yes, if you both mean harm." The second had come to stand at her side after calling a sharp order to the lad to "Watch the other one!"

Adriana looked at their hard faces, seeing deep anxiety in the frowns and set chins. "Sirs, I know not your business here, but I and my apprentice were gathering herbs." She made a point of glancing at both blades winking in the moonlight. "Unarmed as I am, I cannot do you much harm."

They looked almost ready to agree. One even lowered his sword when the lad called, "Sirs! It is Pait! Pait sworn to Lord Mark! And he is badly hurt!"

That one sheathed his blade, but only to grab her by the arm. "Who are you, woman, that you've injured one of our own?"

She'd been right in her guess, but hoped she'd live long enough to explain. By the way he shook her and dragged her toward the fire, she wondered. The other kept his sword ready, his face harsher than the first—if that were possible.

But they were dragging her toward Pait. "You are sure 'tis him?" the second one asked the lad.

"Indeed sir...but he is grievously wounded."

"Woman," the first one said, dragging her further, "you deserve to die for this!"

"First make sure you know what 'this' is!" she said, looking him in the eye. "Pait is wounded, yes. He was tortured by Astrian soldiers. The clean bandages and salves he needs are on the goat you allowed to run away!"

They hesitated, eying each other and then her, as if judging the possible truth in her words.

"He's bleeding, sirs!" the lad called, his voice tight with panic.

"Is no matter." Pait's voice was weak and tired. Adriana broke from the man's grip and ran to Pait's side. He was sitting up. Just. His face pale in the firelight, and yes, he was bleeding. The fall had opened one of the abrasions on his face. Blood was trickling down his cheek. "Is nothing," he insisted. True, compared with his other injuries it was trivial.

"It still needs care, Pait, and..."

"Indeed, it is Pait!" one of the men exclaimed. "But why is he garbed as a girl, woman?"

Adriana permitted herself to glare. "I had no boy's clothes at hand. He was naked when I found him and I dressed him as best I could!" Dear Goddess, protect her!

"Lord Drave," Pait said, looking at the one who'd grabbed her arm and still looked ready to bodily throw her back into the woods. "This lady indeed rescued me. We were on our way to Merridale to warn my lord."

"Is that so?"

His bearing and dress reminded her of Mark, and the party of three matched his description. "You are an auditor from the emperor too, sir?"

"What know you of auditors, woman?" the other one demanded.

"My name is Adriana. I know little of auditors, sir, but know one who traveled this way, and from what I learned from Pait, I fear treachery is at work." She drew herself up straight. "You, sir, know my name, but I lack that advantage."

"That is Lord Drave of Bendholt," Pait said, looking at the first one, "and Lord Carne of Carne. I am remiss, lady, in my presentation. And they are one of the emperor's audit parties."

"Pait, you are remiss in nothing! And your cut needs cleaning. After all your hurts, to have a small cut fester..." But first, she needed her packs.

"Allat will find Hareth, lady. He can run faster than ever I could, even with good feet." Pait was trying to reassure her! He was the one hurt.

"Aye." The one called Carne of Carne still loomed over her, looking very ready to draw his sword again. "And I would like to know how you came by those injuries, lad."

Now she did glare at him. "I told you! It was your soldiers!"

Pait obviously disapproved of snarling at lords. "It was at Fort Antin, Lord Carne. My lord Mark sent me there to ask for fresh horses, but Captain Quel took the sigil and demanded where Lord Mark was going. When I refused to tell, he—" Pait broke off, but only momentarily. "They forced me to tell them." He hung his head as if in shame.

"Ye Gods!" Drave of Bendholt roared. "Villainy among the trusted!" He looked at Adriana, his expression just a little less harsh. "And how, lady, do you come into this?"

"She saved my life!"

That rendered them both speechless for several seconds. Allat returned just then, red-faced from running, but with

Hareth and his load intact. Adriana therefore chose to ignore the question in favor of fetching a waterleather, a linen cloth and salve.

Tending Pait's cut took just minutes. All three were waiting now. The men were looming over her and Allat squatted on his haunches, staring in ill-disguised horror at the bandages on Pait's feet.

"Fetch ham and bread, Allat," Drave said. "We might as well breakfast since sleep seems done for the night."

So, once again, Adriana ate Astrian food, and in return, she and Pait told their parts of the story. They were halfway through when the brightening light gave everyone a clear sight of Pait's injuries.

"Dear Gods!" Carne muttered. "How could they do that—and to a boy?"

"He survived. Is that not what matters?" Drave said. "Our concerns are confirmed."

"Yes, my lords." Pait then asked, "Why are you here and not on the seaboard side?"

"By chance," Drave replied. "We paused by the Inn at Four Cross and heard that just a day before a traveler had died there. The sheriff was fussing over who would pay for the burial. Seemed he died a pauper, but his board had been paid in advance for eight weeks. We were ready to ignore it and pass on, but the sheriff enlisted us to arbitrate. Carne went up to look at the body for valuables or clothes to be sold to pay the costs, and found Karrel.

"We arranged for his funeral and learned from the host that Lord Mark had paid for his board and care. We also found that Karrel had had visitors—the same afternoon he had been found dead. We resolved to find Lord Mark and ascertain the truth. We knew he was headed for Merridale so we altered course. We feared you, Pait, and Lord Mark may have been waylaid too. We know what happened to you. It is treachery indeed, but is Lord Mark safe?"

"Three days ago he was," Adriana said. Anything could occur in three days.

"Aye." Carne gave her an appraising look. "And what is Lord Mark to you, lady?"

The man I love. The one I can never have. "He was lost in the mist. I directed him back on the path."

"Indeed."

She would not have believed it either. "He rode away after the mist lifted." Long after. How she wished he'd never gone now...

"Lady, you live in the forest?" Carne seemed unable to credit it, but she had emerged from it, and Pait corroborated most of her story.

"Lady," Drave said, "if we take your word, Mark will be in Merridale by now, facing mayhap treachery and treason, and we are still two days' hard ride away."

"Maybe not." But could she...

"Lady, we know the distance," Carne said.

"Over the road, it takes two days. Pait and I were traveling another way."

It took both men a long minute to catch her meaning. Allat caught it in seconds. "Through the forest, Pait?"

"Ye Gods!" Carne gasped.

Drave stared in silence, but his eyes showed clearly what he thought of the possibility.

"One hears tales of men wandering in the forest and coming out not knowing their names or past," Carne went on.

Adriana hoped it was not yet light enough to show her reddened face.

"There are many tales," she said carefully. "But I live there and have since I was a girl. Lord Mark of Windhaw entered the forest and left unharmed."

"I traveled through it twice," Pait added. "I've taken no hurt there. My harm was at Fort Antin where I went for help!"

"Is there truly a faster way?" Carne asked. He seemed to be the leader.

Adriana nodded. "Much faster—we would have been through the forest by now if I had not turned off the path when I smelled your fire."

They were torn. That was as clear as the brightening sky. If only they would agree to let her guide them, it would save a day. What was she doing? Proposing to show Astrians a path through the forest! Sweet Rache! What next? But if they were men such as Mark... They were certainly his comrades. And if they were to combine their swords and her magick...

"Lady," Carne spoke—she had been right, he was the leader. "I will follow you through the forest, but I will not command my recorder or my page to come."

"I'll come! If Pait isn't afraid then I am not!" Allat sprung to his feet in indignation.

"You think I have less courage than you, coz?" Drave asked. "Mark is in danger. We cannot hold back."

Belongings packed and fire buried, they set off. Pait rode the horse that Carne led, the others led their own mounts, and all followed Adriana and Hareth, who seemed almost as relieved as Pait that he had another mount.

No one spoke. The magick of the woods around them impressed even the tall Astrians. Allat, Adriana was sure, would have run the other way if he had not committed to being as brave as Pait. But follow her they did, and by late afternoon, they emerged from the fringes of the great forest and saw the town of Merridale surrounded by rich farmland.

"Ye Gods!" Carne muttered. "Indeed it is a far swifter way." He looked back at the dark woods they'd crossed. "If we had a road this way, it would save many days' travel."

"No!" she all but shouted. "The forest is sacred to our Goddesses. You Astrians killed us and took our land, for mercy's sake, leave us our forest!"

Dear Rache, she had spoken too sharply! They all stared at her. Fear and something else deep in their eyes. "Lady Adriana," Carne said, "if you so resent us, why feign aid?"

Curse her too-ready tongue! It was only fatigue and worry that had caused her outburst. "I do not feign aid. I offered to guide you through the forest, and guide you I did. I helped Pait because, unlike your compatriots, I would not abandon an injured child."

"And why this concern to find Lord Mark?"

Sweet Rache! An Astrian inquisition! "I go at Pait's behest. He is anxious about his master. He feared he had betrayed him and I knew, by chance, where Mark of Windhaw was headed. Did we not tell you this before?"

"Aye," Drave agreed. "But how Mark came to be deep in the forest...?" He shook his head.

This line of questioning had to stop. "Best ask him when you find him."

"And we won't find him by debating here," Carne said. He looked across to the town. "If we rode hard, we could reach the gates before sundown. Pait could ride with me but, lady..." He looked at Adriana. "Would you ride with Lord Drave?"

She shook her head. "And who would Hareth ride with? No, that will not work."

"You have a better plan, lady?" Carne sounded skeptical.

"Mayhap." Dear Rache, let them listen. "If we enter the town together, we will get noticed. Astrian auditors do not travel with the likes of me. But if we enter separately, who would notice?"

"So, lady...?"

She pointed toward the curving road. "You could join the road, the way anyone would expect you to come. You can enter the town freely and with little notice. Pait and I will follow. It will be late dusk by the time we get there, but I am known at the gates, and no one remarks on a woman and a goat."

They were both silent, considering her suggestion. "What," Drave asked, "happens after we are in Merridale?"

"Does that not depend on what we find? If we are there ahead of Quel's men, you find Lord Mark and warn him..." She would not consider the possibility that they were too late.

"Aye, but best we not announce ourselves to the master. If there is treachery, it will not help if we are seized, too. We cannot ask for official lodging." Drave shook his head.

"There is an inn at the lower end of the town called the Demented Hare. Host Martten is an honest, decent man. Why not hire rooms from him? I always lodge there and planned to stop there with Pait."

"Would serve," Drave agreed. "We could make enquiries and see what, if anything, has transpired."

"It means leaving Pait behind," Carne said.

"Aye, but Lady Adriana is right. If he is with her, it will not awaken interest, but if we rode in with him dressed as he is now, the sentries would think we'd abducted a village lass."

Carne's look of shock could not have been feigned. Astrians surprised her more and more. "Seems best," he said, "that we follow your suggestions, lady. But I will not rest easy until I see you both again."

And she would not rest easy until she knew Mark was safe and she had returned to her haven. It would weigh heavy to lose Pait, but there was no question in her heart that he would return to Mark. Carne lifted Pait down from the horse and set him on Hareth's back. Neither were pleased at the change. Minutes later, they cantered off toward the road. Adriana had never thought she would miss Astrians, but miss them she did.

"Lady, how long till we reach this inn?" Pait asked. He'd scarce said a word for hours. Adriana hoped that he'd slept as they'd crossed the forest.

"We'll be there before dark. There are narrow paths across the farms that we can take. Tonight you'll sleep in a warm attic. Host Martten's wife keeps a good kitchen, and they are always generous."

CR SO

Tonight was no different.

Tam the Hostler met her at the stable gate. "Early this year, Mistress Adriana."

"Yes, a change is good for all. You have space for Hareth?"

"Always! And you have the herbs and salves for my rheumatism?"

"As always!"

Adriana had planned to ask for news once Pait was asleep, but before then Host Martten himself climbed to her attic, a frown between his bushy eyebrows. "Mistress, I don't know what brought you here out of season—my wife thanks the Goddess you did for replenishing her stores—but I must warn you something has left me uneasy."

Chapter Seven

Adriana's throat tightened. "What?"

Host Martten shook his head, grasping his fleshy jowls with a large hand. "I dunno rightly, but these two men are staying here. They have good horses and a page with them, and they look like officials, or at least men of stature." She exhaled. They had to be here—and safe. "After they dined, they lingered in the taproom and started asking young Jinny about a peddler herbalist, traveling with a young lass."

So that was how they pegged her—a peddler! "Two men in dark capes, riding a tall roan and a gray, the boy on a dappled pony?" she asked.

"Aye!" He looked even more dubious.

"No call for uneasiness, Host. They are travelers we met on the way. They were lost and I directed them to the road."

Relief softened his face. "Ah! I'm right glad to hear that, what with the trouble we've had in town. I don't want any more."

"What trouble?"

The crease reappeared between Martten's eyes. His eyebrows all but met this time. "You missed a few rough days, mistress—be thankful. A band of soldiers arrived two days ago."

Her throat went tight. "They delivered a proclamation from the emperor. Seems illegal auditors are operating in his name."

Now she almost stopped breathing. She made herself inhale and exhale. "Indeed."

"Aye! And then it turns out one is already here! He was tried yesterday. Swift justice, praise to the heavens."

"He was found guilty?"

"Of course! No doubt about it. Why, I left the taproom to Jinny and sat in the council chamber myself. Oh, he protested his innocence he did, claimed he was sent by the emperor, even produced a sigil. That damned him further. They then accused him of high treason and he will be hanged at sunset tomorrow."

She heard Pait's gasp, but dared not look sideways at him. Best treat this as casual news. "Any other happenings?"

"Not much. Still talk of a new bridge and schools, but I doubt the emperor has time for outposts like this. My lass Hanny is to be married come Michaelmas. She's pledged to Gram, the butcher's son..." Adriana let him continue, although impatient to meet with Carne and Drave.

Finally, Martten paused, then suggested, "Well, mistress, if you and the lass would care to sup, my wife has a good mutton stew..."

"Oh, please," Pait interrupted. They had not stopped to eat all day.

"Yes, little missy." Host Martten smiled. "We'll send a bowl up here, and not forget you."

It was how he always served Adriana, saving her from the stares in the taproom. "After supping, I would talk awhile with the other travelers. They were courteous, and..."

"Mistress, they cannot come up here!" Martten objected.

Oh dear, she'd outraged his sense of propriety.

"Not that I doubt you, mistress, I know you of old, but there would be talk, and this is not the Wild Boar." An inn of dubious repute near the garrison.

"I cannot enter the taproom."

His plump mouth drew up like his brows as he pondered that one. "Tell you what. If they sat on my back veranda, and you joined them there for a wee while, 'twould offend no one, and you'd not be bothered by the company."

Would work.

Her biggest stumbling block was insisting Pait remain behind. He begged to be included, but when she pressed the point that she needed him rested the next day he grudgingly acquiesced. After a full bowl of mutton stew and fresh barley bread, he was ready to drop. Adriana redressed his feet and fingers, put salve on his still-livid bruises and cuts and brewed him a tisane to ease the aches and help him sleep.

Gathering the soiled bandages, she descended the back stairs. She stopped in the kitchen to toss her burden on the fire, and after a word or two with Martten's wife Sarral, Adriana went out onto the veranda.

Both men rose at her approach. When she saw Allat was not there, she knew she'd done right to leave Pait upstairs.

"You have heard the news, Lady Adriana?" Carne asked.

"That Mark of Windhaw is accused and condemned? Yes. Host Martten told me."

"Ye Gods!" Drave muttered. "That villain Quel! He must have dispatched horse soldiers as soon as he'd wrung the knowledge from Pait." He lifted the ewer, poured a mug of cider and offered it to Adriana. "We have nothing to celebrate, lady, but 'tis a fine cider."

She took the cup in both hands, nodding her thanks.

"What can we do?" Carne asked the world in general and the night around them. "If we had an army, we could fight, but no doubt we, too, are named traitor. I knew. We all knew there was opposition to the emperor's will, but on this scale..."

"It is just one garrison, is it not?" she asked

"One garrison, half an army. What difference against two? I'd storm them myself but would not expose Allat or Pait to more ill treatment."

Dejected was not the word for their mien. And she'd thought Astrians were always arrogant and insolent. She had learned so much the past few days. She sipped the cider—it was, as always, cool and smooth. Host Martten kept many of the old ways and a fine pressing was one of them.

"We must do something. One of us approach the master and test the outcome. I'll go," Drave said. "If I, too, am accused, then flee with Allat and head for Fort Dalban. My cousin Gret is commander. He is loyal."

"Dalban is three days' hard ride away. Mark—and you most likely—would hang before we could get there." Carne closed his fingers so tightly around his mug, she expected him to dent the metal.

"It can't be hopeless," Drave insisted.

Carne snorted with disgust. "What are our choices? Sit by and let him hang? Or join him?"

"There is a third choice."

They both stared at her. "Indeed, what is that?" Carne asked. "Storming the garrison?"

"No...rescuing Mark of Windhaw."

They'd looked less astounded when Pait had charged out of the forest at them.

"Impossible!" Carne snapped. "Two against the garrison and half the assembled town!"

"Three," she said. "Five, counting the lads."

"Still suicidal," Drave said. "And putting the lads at risk is criminal! It will not happen!"

They both all but snarled at her.

"If we had a detachment of loyal soldiers, yes," Drave said, "but what can we hope to achieve but cause a few innocent bystanders to be trampled to death in the stampede to arrest us."

"Lady, I know you mean well—" Carne began.

"You are both wrong." While they stared, irritation and worry darkening their eyes, she went on. "We have more strength than you know." She took a deep breath. She could be signing her own death warrant. If they denounced her, she'd swing beside Mark, but... "Pait spoke truer than he imagined when he asked if I were a witch." Now that she had them stunned into muteness, she forged on. "I have power and knowledge that I can and will use to help. The scaffold is set up on the open ground by the river. I can raise a mist strong enough to obscure and confuse everyone. You can use the confusion to rescue Mark."

"And then?" Drave asked.

He was not discounting it. "Then you take him and Pait to safety, to the fort your cousin commands. Can't he keep you safe and send a message to your emperor?"

"You make it sound like a simple task, lady. But there will be crowds at the hanging—soldiers, armed guards," Carne said.

Simple? These Astrians had no idea! "Not simple, but not impossible. What other choices are there? Sending for help?

You yourself said Mark would be hanged before the message arrives. Storming the garrison?" They both frowned at her.

"Lady," Drave began, "what you propose is blasphemy."

"Maybe, but letting Mark hang is a greater one!" Carne said. "Seems to me the emperor was right in suspecting irregularities in these parts, and our commission was to note and report."

"Yes." Drave looked at Adriana. "Lady, can you truly raise a mist thick enough to hide us?"

"Yes." It would leave her wan and exhausted, but she could hide until she recovered, and Mark would be safe.

There was little else to say. Carne agreed to hire extra horses and meet her in the marketplace late afternoon.

CR ꙮ

Adriana spent the next morning selling herbs and potions from a hired stall in the market. To not set up shop would have caused questions about her early arrival, and the marketplace was the hub for news and gossip.

And gossip there was.

Her stall was squeezed between a tinker and a butcher selling sausages and hams. Just the smell of them brought back memories of the meal with Mark. Dear Goddess! Why had she fallen in love with a man she could never have? Or could she? Had he not promised to return? Mayhap he felt the same, or at least held a fondness for her. But how could she love what she'd sworn to destroy? How could she harm a man whose aim was to right wrongs? Why...

"Ye have a potion for the shaking sickness, mistress?"

Torn from her agonizing by the young man's question, Adriana reminded herself why she was here. "Indeed I have. For a child or an adult?"

Minutes later, the young man wandered off with a quantity of ground glarraroot in a paper twist. But more to the point, she'd learned that the hanging at dusk was to be the spectacle of the year.

The sausage man to her left confirmed the news. "Aye, we'll not do much trade once they bring him out. They'll all flock down to the water's edge." He shook his head. "My son's going down there to sell food to the crowds. It's not every day we see a hanging."

"Why this time?"

He shrugged. "It's said he came as a spy, a scout for a revolt to overthrow the master." He spat on the cobblestones by his feet. "So, to protect us, we have extra soldiers quartered in the town. True, the garrison will order more provisions from the merchants, but who's to say when they will pay?" He broke off to turn to a housewife with a large basket over her arm.

No two thoughts about it, rescuing Mark would be just the beginning. Had Quel sent extra troops to take over the town? Was he in collusion with the master? She had no doubt about her ability to raise the mist. That, to her mind, was the simple part. Getting away would be harder. But hadn't Drave and Carne agreed to take care of that?

It seemed they trusted her to do her part...

Waiting was hard. Waiting and keeping Pait's spirits up was harder still. And waiting and behaving as if this were any ordinary day to trade was nigh on impossible. But she had to do it. She set Pait to measuring out portions of herbs and roots and sealing them in twists, and resolved to shut up shop early. If trade would slack off as the sausage seller predicted, why stay? Leaving early would not occasion much comment, and she needed time to pray before performing magick of such dimensions.

CR ℬ

The shouts of the soldiers could be heard across the market square as they ordered townspeople to clear the way. Bodies jostled each other and several pushed toward Adriana's rented stall. The sausage seller grabbed Pait and lifted him behind the stall. "Best not let the soldiers see her," he said. "Even a crippled girl's not safe from some of them."

"Stay behind the stall, Pait," Adriana said. It would be even worse if someone grabbed him or pushed him over and saw he wasn't a girl.

Pait sat down on an upturned box and leaned against the stall. He looked tired, and despite her best efforts, Adriana was sure his wounds still pained him. She slipped him a sliver of andine, and he smiled as he put it in his mouth.

The noise grew worse, the crowd rowdier. But they parted for the approach of a double file of soldiers and a cart. Seeing the man in the cart, Adriana thanked every Goddess in creation that Pait was out of sight. These people were fiends. Each turn of the squeaky wheels brought the cart closer, but even half a market square away Adriana saw the dirt and dark in the fair hair and the livid bruises on his face and shoulders. As they reached level with the old tinker's stall, a handful of dirt hit Mark in the face. The force caused him to turn away. And as he glanced up, his eyes met Adriana's. She should thank Rache for the gaze devoid of all recognition, but instead it ripped at her heart. He knew her not! Of course not, she'd taken that away! It was for the best. If Mark recognized her, who knew what trouble might ensue? But her heart tore as she watched his naked back disappear in the crowd and nothing, ever, would erase from her memory the bloody whip marks cut across his back.

Why? Why ask? To force information as they had from Pait. Had they burned his feet too? Ripped out his toenails? She shuddered at the thought. Please, Rache, not. He was still standing, wasn't he? But what if the rest of him was as beaten and bloodied as his chest?

"Let it not fret you, mistress! It is only an old wife's tale about meeting a condemned man's eye!" She smiled at the butcher's concern. The honest trader had no notion, praise the Five Goddesses!

"I know." She forced herself to nod and smile while her heart twisted and tore. She gave another glance to the departing crowd. "You spoke truly about customers leaving."

"For some of us, mistress." He nodded toward Carne who stood in front of her stall.

"Sir?"

"Mistress, I came to enquire as to your supply of pain easers."

He'd seen Mark's beaten body too! "I have a goodly supply, sir. Whatever your needs may be."

He looked at her, a furrow between his brows. "Lady, if you would bring an ample portion and come and see my horse, I would be in your debt." Did she look like a horse doctor? "Lady, I beg you. Mere minutes are all I need..."

It had to be about Mark! "I will come, sir." Stopping only seconds to ask Pait to watch the stall, she walked with Carne round the corner. As she expected, his horse was nowhere in sight. "Lady Adriana, they have changed the execution."

Mercy? Commutation? No! Not from the look on Carne's face. The flicker of hope extinguished. "How so?"

"I think the gathering crowd alarmed the master of the town, and after a group of youths set a fire in the river meadow, he ordered the hanging proceed as soon as the hangman and the priest could be fetched."

Dear Rache! She had no time to pray or meditate or prepare. Not now! "We must get Pait! What about the horses?"

"Drave and Allat have them beyond the bridge. Lady, can you do this?"

"Is the river still accesible?" He nodded, his eyes dark with worry. "Then I can work a spell, but we have no time to tarry. And let us hope the hangman is delayed."

She ran back to the stall and found Pait talking earnestly to a fat housewife. "Mistress," he said as Adriana approached, "this good wife needs a potion for..."

She didn't pause to listen to the good wife's ills. "Pait, we must go!" While he stared, she turned to the woman. "A pardon, good wife, but I have an urgent call—a man is dying!" Carne picked up Pait, looked at Adriana, then the stall. "The stall matters not!" What use were any of her potions if she failed to help Mark?

They ran toward the lower end of town, leaving behind a perplexed tinker, a curious butcher and an irate good wife.

Halfway down the hill, Adriana slowed. Carne stopped. "Why delay, lady? Do you tire?"

She shook her head to save her panting breath. "You must get Pait to safety. We can run, but he cannot." And there would be the chase to end all chases when Mark's escape was discovered.

"I'll put him and Allat on a horse together."

Pait looked dubious, but it was more from rebellion than fear. "I had hoped to help save my lord."

"You will by obeying orders," Carne said.

And at that, Pait gave no more argument. "I'll be back at once," Carne told Adriana, and disappeared toward the bridge.

She was alone with only her well-honed powers to aid her. Were they enough? Raising a mist and sending it across the forest edges was one thing, calling up a river to engulf the town in fog was another. And what if her actions angered Rache? No, they would not. This was true revenge against the marauders. Mark's hand would strike the blow, but only if she freed him.

She followed the knot of people down the hill and out the city gates. The gibbet stood like a gaunt skeleton in the early afternoon sunshine. Below the town, the wide Merri meandered across the fertile meadows. Adriana elbowed her way though the crowd, hoping that Drave had Pait to safety and that they would all meet, as agreed, just below the bridge. With the amount of mist she hoped to raise, the river would be shallow enough to ford. Did she have the skills for this? Dear Rache! She had to!

She did not want to look at Mark again. She dreaded meeting his eyes that were utterly devoid of recognition, but she needed to see exactly where he was. So she edged her way toward the platform. Soldiers surrounded him, but she saw enough to see the contusions on his face and the marks of beating on his naked chest. Before today, she'd seen that chest naked and had rested her head on the warm skin to listen to the beating of his heart. Now her own heart twisted in sorrow, hankering for her lost love and the man who would never again look at her with passion.

"Lady?" Carne whispered from behind her. He was there, with Drave.

"Aye," she whispered.

"We are ready," Drave said.

"Pait and Allat?"

"Are mounted, waiting below the bridge with the horses."

She looked up at the fair-haired man standing by the gibbet like a graven statue. "I doubt he can walk that far."

"No need to, lady," Drave said in her ear. "We have horses nearby and just wait for your effort."

Then they should have it. She turned and looked at them—honorable, noble Astrians. And with her back to the finest one of all, she nudged her way through the crowd toward the riverbank, stopping just paces from where the two boys waited.

A few paces out in the river, there was a large rock. Taking off her shoes and tying them to her girdle, she gathered her skirts in her hand and waded out. She was surrounded by the Merri's sweet, swirling water. Rache's own cool stream fed into this river. Adriana felt the magick flow around her feet and prayed, summoning all her power and strength. As the mist rose around her feet, she drove it toward shore and called up more and more.

At first, it was mere swirls of vapor, but as her concentration grew, mist turned to fog. Then the fog became a great cloud that rolled toward the town, toward the crowd, toward the gibbet, and the man she loved who would never know her again.

She kept up the fog, pouring it thicker and heavier toward the town until the river slowed and cries of consternation reached her from the soldiers and the crowd.

She had done her part. Now it was up to Carne and Drave. But could they find their way in the fog?

Dear Rache! If they got trapped in the town! She waded toward the horses. The mist agitated them, but she sang them calm. She wished she had her pipe to call the other horses. There was the sound of hooves, muffled by the mist, and then Pait called, "Mistress, you must mount. They come!"

Mount a horse? Impossible! "No, you go." She had thought to double back to the town and reclaim Hareth and her belongings. But...

Hooves thundered down on them. Mark rode behind Carne, with Drave leading. "Lady, mount!" Drave called. "We must away—already the fog thins."

"I cannot ride!" she called. "I will—" But her words ended in a gasp as Drave reached down and swept her up behind him. Her words of protest were silenced as they thundered across the river, Pait and Allat a little ahead of them, the water splashing around the animals' hooves like a great cold tide. Adriana clung to Drave's back in terror, forcing her mind to maintain the fog behind them.

They galloped across the meadows, leaping hedges and ditches, until the uproar behind them died. Adriana glanced back as they entered the forest. The mist was clearing but still thick enough for them to enter the trees unseen.

"Guide us here, lady," Carne asked. "You know the way."

"Let me down first!" The feel of the forest earth under her bare feet was a joy. Here she was safe and anchored. She untied her shoes from her waist and put them back on her feet. The others dismounted, all except Pait. Even Mark stood, a cloak now covering his marks and scars.

"Lady," he said, his voice tight as his chest rose and fell. "I know you not, but I owe you my life. I will be forever in your debt."

"No, sir. Bring justice to this land, establish your university where Astrian and Baremes share knowledge and you will have repaid me a hundredfold."

"Why would you risk yourself for this? You did call up that mist, did you not? You wrought magick to aid my friends in their endeavor."

"Yes, I used magick. I could not conjure up a battalion of armed men, but mist I could call."

He stared at her, his blue eyes all but piercing her heart at the utter lack of recognition. "Lady, such graciousness for a stranger."

That, unfortunately, caught everyone's ears.

"But, Mark—" Carne began.

"We thought—" Drave said.

"But sir, you did meet her. In the forest," Pait said. "She had your seal—look."

She'd thought her heart could twist no more. She was wrong. Pait turned the pocket of her cut-down cloak inside out and revealed the silver button. Her fingers clasped the ring under her shift. That he must not see.

Mark stared at the silver button, incomprehension still clouding his face as a crease appeared between his eyes. He reached for the button, pulled it off the cloth and looked at the polished silver in his hand. "Indeed it is mine. It bears my family's oatlen tree." He looked back at Adriana. "How came you by this?"

"I found it on the rocks by a stream near where I live. After I found Pait, he recognized it as his lord's. We went to find you, met Drave and Carne and Allat and," she shrugged as if to make light of all this, "we found you."

"Snatched me from the hangman, in truth and substance. I had the rope around my neck when Carne's knife cut the noose."

"I thank the Five Goddesses he was in time." And would until her last breath.

Pait was obviously confused; this did not quite jibe with what she'd told him. She prayed he would not contradict. "We must move on," she said. "I will show you the way through the forest so you will emerge close to Fort Dalban."

It took hours—they followed slowly as Mark was injured. Darkness fell, but at her insistence, they continued until near dawn, emerging at the far rim of the forest. "The fort is but a few hours along that way," she said, pointing to road stretching over the meadows where wild beast grazed in a widespread flock. "May Rache speed your work."

"Lady," this time it was Carne of Carne who spoke, "will you not come with us?"

Go with them and suffer the blank, unknowing eyes of the man she loved more than life itself? She shook her head. "No, sir. I belong in the forest. My mission is to serve Rache." Though she'd have to find a new way to honor the Goddess. Never could she let another man touch her now. "As you're sworn to serve your emperor. Go with the blessing of the Five Goddesses and your Five Gods."

Mark stepped forward and grasped her elbow with his hand—it was the way Astrians greeted each other—and accepting the honor, she grasped his elbow. The touch of his flesh sent memories rushing like a bitter flood. Never could she forget him! To the end of her days, she'd remember the sweet caress of his mouth on her lips, on her breasts, on her skin, between her legs. Blood rushed to her face as her body remembered his hard cock inside. She swallowed and looked up into his unknowing eyes. "I wish you the speed on your journey, Lord Mark of Windhaw, and may justice ever be your loyal servant."

He nodded. "At your behest, lady, I will pursue justice in my emperor's cause."

"And build that university?"

"If I have to lift the stones with my own hands."

Tears pricked behind her eyelids as the weight of his ring hung heavy round her neck. She rejected the temptation to draw it out and declare her love, offer him the proof of what they'd shared. To what avail would that revelation be? He had no memory of her. Her lover knew her not.

Carne and Drave offered her the same farewell salute. Allat bowed and Pait made the best effort he could with a crutch and his still bound foot.

"Lady, I owe you my life," he said.

"Use it wisely then, Pait. Life is precious." She smiled to conceal the misery inside.

Parting was not that easy, but at last, with her insistence that speed was of the essence, they left. She stood in the rim of the trees and watched them go. Pait turned at a distance and waved. She waved back, knowing he could not see her among the trees. From Mark, there was no sign. How could there be? He did not know her.

That thought carried her a distance into the forest before misery engulfed her. She knelt on the loam and wept, praying the forest floor would open up and swallow her and her sorrow.

Chapter Eight

Adriana sobbed until she slept, worn out by despair. Her energy was drained by the magick she'd wrought and her body was fatigued by the strains of travel and lost sleep. When she woke, it was daylight.

What now? Hareth and her goods remained in Merridale. Host Martten would take care of Hareth and her wares she could replace. She would not return to Merridale—not yet. But could she go back to the shrine and the ever-present memories of Mark? No! She was not that strong. To Aenwath and visit Eadyyl and Eadwyn? They had succored her before when her heart was all but rent from her body with sorrow.

She stood up, brushed leaf mold and dirt off her clothes, picked up the leather satchel of food and provisions the Astrians had insisted on leaving with her and set her feet toward her mentors' haven.

The sight of their welcoming faces and open arms all but undid her. She hugged them both, sat on a flat rock in front of their cave and wept in both their arms. "Eadyyl, Eadwyn," she sobbed. "I am so torn, I cannot think!"

"No need." Eadyyl's old hands stroked her head as she held her close. "You are too exhausted to think. Rest and when you awaken then we will talk."

Adriana gladly sipped the tisane Eadwyn had prepared. As she lay down on the sleeping furs, Adriana thought herself too frazzled to sleep. She was wrong. The soothing drink did its work and before long she was sleeping deeply enough to be oblivious to the concerned whispers between her mentors.

CR SD

She woke after sleeping the day around. She was stiff, aching, and heavy-headed, but the sight of the old familiar rock roof overhead, the sounds of Eadyyl humming in the sunshine and the cascade on the rocks outside all took Adriana back, for a few moments, to her childhood and the love she'd known from her foster mothers. For a few moments, it was as if she were a child again, safe in the deep forest. But child she was not! And had not been for years. Her heartbreak was a woman's heartbreak.

"Good morrow, child," Eadyyl said as Adriana emerged into the light.

She would always be "child" to these old women—and old they were now. Eadyyl's welcoming smile added even more creases to her lined face. Adriana hugged Eadyyl close, but the closeness only underscored the frail old body. "I have stayed away too long," Adriana said. "I have neglected you both."

"No, child. We have our work and you have yours. We both serve our Goddesses. Now, you go and bathe, my dear. You smell of travel and turmoil." Not to be wondered at! Her life had been nothing but for the past few days! "Go to the springs and we will prepare food to break your fast. We have fowl now. Eadwyn clips their wings so they cannot fly far. She is gone now to gather eggs for you."

"I have food, too." Adriana went back into the cave for the satchel Carne of Carne had insisted she take. "This, in itself, is part of my story. Take what you need, and when I am washed, I will tell you all."

Adriana went to their warm spring. It was larger than hers and the stonework even finer. How Mark would exclaim at the sight of this! She shut her eyes. Mark, and the love they'd shared, was past. She had taken herself from him. Helped save him, yes, and now she was back in the world where she belonged. She looked down at her legs and feet. Eadyyl had been right, she badly needed a wash. By the edge of the pool next to the folded drying cloths was a clean shift and a worn but mended gown and a twisted girdle.

Adriana dropped her long-worn clothes to the ground and leapt into the pool, closing her eyes as the warm water splashed her face. She then dipped her head fully under the water. How wonderful it felt! She made herself banish the memories of bathing with Mark. She would lose her mind if she dwelt on the unattainable. She scrubbed her skin with sand and immersed herself in the water time after time, emerging clean and refreshed. She dried off quickly, pulling on the clean clothes and rubbing her hair dry before tugging out the tangles and knots with a wooden comb.

She was clean, hungry and ready to face her mentors, her mothers—by fact if not by blood. Indeed the memory of her own mother was so faint she could scarce remember her face. So much had happened since those long gone days. She was no longer a scared child but woman—a woman who'd saved the life of the man she loved and was now condemned to live without him.

So be it.

She braided her hair, tying the end with a twisted thread as she walked through the cave.

Eadwyn had returned and embraced Adriana. "It is an answer to prayer to have you with us again. Come, I found eggs and Eadyyl has heated the cooking stones." She had also roasted roots and warmed the ham from Adriana's satchel. "You must tell us how you came by this meat. A luxury indeed, child."

"The ham is just the end of what I have to tell." Adriana sat down between them. "My heart has been torn."

"Hearts mend," Eadwyn said, "and most sorrows ease when shared." She handed Adriana a trencher of warm food and a mug of tisane. "Let us eat and you tell what has disturbed you so."

Adriana ate. Their plates were scraped and the fire down to ashes and embers by the time she had finished. Eadwyn had been right. The hurt had eased with telling. But now Adriana feared their judgment for compromising her oath.

For a long time, they said nothing. They just sat on the grass as the birds sang overhead. Maybe she should stay here with them forever. But no, she was no longer a child to be cosseted and cared for. She was a woman and must face life— alone.

"You love him, Adriana, don't you?" Eadwyn asked.

Adriana nodded. "If what I feel is love, I love him."

"What do you feel?" Eadyyl asked.

"When I was with him, I felt complete. Not just the physical pleasure—much as that astounded me—it was as if he filled what had been missing in me." And now she would live bereft for the rest of her days.

"Do you not think he knows that too?" Eadwyn asked.

"He does not remember me! I took that away from him!"

"He may not remember you, Adriana, but do you think he could forget your joining? The joy you shared and gave each other?"

"What am I to do?"

"Go back to Rache, tend your goats and think. The answer will come."

She wanted a guidepost, a signal. But looking at the two women who'd loved her since they had rescued her from the outskirts of her village, she knew the answer was not here. "Will you pray that I find direction?"

"How could we not, child," Eadwyn said.

"Your heart knows the direction," Eadyyl added. "Just look inward."

"The day is fine, the clouds high," Eadwyn said. "You can be back at Rache's springs by nightfall. There, you will find the answer."

Still unsure, but trusting her mentors, Adriana set off and arrived back by moonlight. By the time she walked up the path by the stream toward her cave, she was tired but resolute.

She dropped the satchel inside the cave and went through to the warm pool. She walked around the edge, watching the glimmer of moon on the dark water, remembering.

Eadyyl and Eadwyn insisted her heart knew what to do, but it seemed her heart was too hurt and torn to know anything but pain. What could she do but petition Rache? Adriana climbed the escarpment until she reached her perch high above the pool. From here she could look toward the plain where she'd seen Mark of Windhaw first approach and back into the forest that had sheltered her all these years. She sat back against the rock and looked out into the night, praying for guidance. She nodded, dozed and forced herself awake. Sometimes she dreamed, and sometimes she sensed she was seeing into her past and the deep recesses of her mind.

CR SO

By the time the dawn paled the sky, Adriana had resolved her course.

It took her five days to prepare—to tidy her cave, and neaten the shrine, and gather what provisions she could. She cleaned the sluices of the bathing pool so they would operate in her absence. One day, perhaps, another priestess would come to tend the springs. She packed the last of her belongings and prepared all her remaining herbs and simples. Each night she prayed on the escarpment, and each night, the same answer came.

She loved Mark of Windhaw. And just as she had allied with Astrians to save him, now she must risk all to join him. She took on faith Eadwyn's conviction that he retained the memory of their pleasure.

With the shrine cleansed, she summoned Hareth's mate, Tynda, a bad-tempered ewe. The goat resisted being harnessed and ran off into the forest and refused Adriana's call. Was this an omen? Would she lose Mark, too? It was a temptation to stay safe in the forest. But no. Her heart called her beyond the sheltering trees. Discarding what she could not carry, Adriana shouldered the rest and set off though the forest.

It was another two days before she emerged at the spot where she had watched Mark ride away toward Fort Dalban. She was weary but took her waterleather from her shoulder and drank deep of Rache's water. She washed her face and hands, then stepped out of the shelter of the trees. The herd she'd noticed before still grazed in the fields, beyond them lay a small village, and beyond that the towers of Fort Dalban.

Distances on the plains were deceptive. It was night before she stood before the fort, and all gates were closed. Her request of the sentry to speak to Lord Mark of Windhaw was met with harsh refusal and a swipe of a rifle butt. She bit back her tears and anger as she retreated and found shelter a distance away in a barn. But she wept bitter tears amongst the straw. To come this close and be refused! But in the morning, the gates would be open. No doubt even soldiers feared the night.

Morning found the gates flung open. As she approached, she glimpsed activity within—soldiers mounting horses, shouts and commands. Could she perhaps slip in? And then what? How in this bustle would she find Mark? If indeed he was still there. What if he had already left? No! She sensed in her heart he was there, but anxiety tugged at her mind. All was not well.

Indeed not! She was still barred from entering.

This guard was civil. "Regrets, mistress, but we are in readiness for action. No one may enter without authorization."

She closed her fingers around the gold ring that still hung around her neck. "I carry the seal of Mark of Windhaw," she said, holding out the ring.

"I can only admit with the emperor's sigil, mistress. It is my orders." From inside came the sound of more shouts and the noise of scores of harnesses and hooves as men mounted and assembled. "Stand clear, mistress—they ready to leave and will stop for no one."

Resigned, she stood aside as the first horsemen approached. As they neared, she looked up. "Carne of Carne!" she called.

He pulled rein as did the other leaders. One signaled for the column to halt. "Lady Adriana! You are here! By the Gods, it is an answer to prayer."

"How so, Carne of Carne?"

"We have need of your healing skills. Lord Mark..."

"He is ill?"

"Gravely, lady. Would seem he took on a miasma in the master's dungeons. Mark fell ill shortly after we arrived here, and we fear for him."

Her heart stilled, to come this far and... "He is dying?"

"Not if your skills can save him as they saved Pait." He turned to the sentry. "Have Lady Adriana conveyed to Lord Mark's sickroom. She is a renowned healer." Carne leaned in his saddle, grasping her hand and elbow. She sensed astonishment among the others that he used the salute reserved for emperor's men. "I must away, lady. We have five parties of the emperor's horse to impose law and righteousness in these parts. I have temporarily abandoned my audit to soldier, but I beg you, do what you can for my friend."

"I will do everything in my power."

With a wave, he slackened his reins, his mount stepped forward and the entire column passed.

The sentry gave her an appraising look, but remembering his orders, he led her across the wide courtyard, even offering to carry her pack. She was passed onto another soldier with, "Lord Carne's orders. She's a healer come to treat the sick lord."

Finally she was led to a room in the lower part of the tower. There were two beds in the room, one neatly rolled up—the covers folded in military precision, the other tumbled and rough—a man tossing fitfully under the covers. The room smelled of decay and sickness. The windows needed throwing open, but first she crossed the room and looked down at the sleeping face, with lips that muttered nightmares of fever dreams and golden hair drenched and slick with sweat.

Had she tarried too long? Was he dying? Not while she lived and breathed!

She turned at a sound by the door. It was Pait, using just one crutch now, and the bruises on his face much faded. "Lady!" His young face broke into smiles. "You have come to save my lord!"

"Indeed I have, Pait! And I need your help."

Pait still hobbled, but he enlisted another page, Bavel, to help them. Bavel and Pait brought clean bedclothes, drying cloths and a brazier to heat kettles of warm water.

Adriana prepared tisanes, and, when he woke, made Mark take sips as best he could. She washed his body with warm water scented with lavender to ease his fever. As she rubbed the soft cloths over his heated skin, she indulged in the sight of his beautiful body.

Dear Rache! Let him recover so she could know that wondrous cock again.

There were hard days ahead. After Lord Carne's direction, she had no trouble obtaining broth or clean linen or whatever she ordered. Pait and Bavel followed her directions and the looks of wonder on Bavel's face convinced her Pait had embellished the tales of his rescue and Mark's escape from Merridale.

Even the day sergeant who passed the room addressed her as "Lady Adriana of Merridale." And one afternoon, the commander Gret of Allburn appeared, asked after Mark's health, and promised her all the help that lay in his hands to offer. It was, he said, a difficult time—orders from the emperor, miscreants to be confined, even a treasonous fort to be overcome. But no matter...if she needed anything it was hers to command.

She got a bigger room for Mark, with large windows. More air, more light and a fireplace where she could heat water and food without smoke filling the room. But still Mark languished. She dressed Pait's feet. They were near to mended—he could walk without crutches if he kept weight off his heels. And a day later, he and Bavel left to carry a missive to Merridale. She missed the boys, but the commander appointed a soldier named Fanic to fetch and carry for her.

She had all the aid they could give. Mark's condition did not worsen, but neither did it improve. Adriana was at her wit's ends. She prayed to Rache each morning. She even entered the stone church across the courtyard and prayed to whatever Astrian God might be listening. But Mark of Windhaw still muttered in his weakness and fever.

One evening, worn out with anxiety and fatigue, Adriana sat by his bedside, bathing his face with lavender water. Her touch soothed him, that she could see. But she was close to exhaustion after her long watch at his side. Her eyes stung with tiredness and her lids drooped as she looked down at the face of the man she loved—the man who'd shown no sign of recognition all these weary days and nights. Dropping the cloth in the bowl beside her, she stroked his cheek, ran her fingers down his neck and caressed his shoulder. How she longed to feel him close, to lie in his arms as she had in the peace and safety of the shrine. Here in these cold walls, he knew her not, but she knew and loved him. Driven by need and the ache deep in her soul, she lifted the covers and lay down beside him.

Oh! To feel his warm hard body beside hers was utter heaven. The sheer joy of his leg against hers...and the softness of his chest hair under her fingers as she rested her hand over his heart... He might not know her, but she knew him and her heart rejoiced at the touch. Worn out by watching, she slept, caressed by his warmth and her hope.

The guard change before dawn woke her. She lay half-awake and listened to the sounds of boots on cobblestones, brisk commands and the clink of metal. There were more feet and shouts—perhaps another muster leaving or arriving—she did not stir to find out. As the sounds outside quieted, she brushed her lips on Mark's cheek. His flesh was cool! Not fever-heated, but the sweet soft cool of healthy skin. She ran her hand over his forehead and down his chest to his hip. The fever had eased! Rache be praised!

As her fingertips brushed the curls at his groin, he muttered. Hoping to catch his words, she sat up and looked down at him, meeting his eyes. They were no longer as clear and confident as when they'd met first by the stream, but cloudy with illness and confusion.

"Sweet lady," he whispered, his voice hoarse and weak, "are you an angel sent to heal me? My body is weak and my soul weary."

"I am Adriana." She spoke with hope he might remember. "You have been sick."

No light of recognition lit his face; there was only the same soul-weary gaze. "Sweet lady, mayhap you are sent from heaven to aid me. Not only has my body been ill, but my mind is uneasy."

"How so?"

"I have spaces, voids in my thoughts. I have lost what I loved, but cannot even remember what I lost. I pursued my duty, but fell into treacherous hands." His hand grasped hers. "You were one of those who saved me, were you not?" She nodded. "I thought so! That I have not forgotten and my page..." He sat up and looked around.

"Pait left on an errand for the commander. He will return."

"Aye, a noble lad. They tortured him you know...that I remember. But when I look back, much is missing. And most of all, I miss the one I loved."

It was as Eadwyn said. Mark remembered loving, but not her. Could she make him remember her? "You have been fevered," she said, stroking his now-cool forehead. "Let me wash you."

"I'm thirsty," he muttered.

She gave him a cup of Rache's water. She had kept it for drinking, using the water carried in from the well for washing. But now she put the last of Rache's water on to heat. This, she sensed, was her only hope. Rache's sacred water—would it spring his memory?

He smiled, but only in thanks, not recognition. "Lady, you are too good to me. Why spend you time with an ailing auditor?"

"Why would I not? You are honorable and strive for the justice that we Baremes hunger for."

He looked at her. "I had heard you Baremes hated us."

"Once I did. Until I learned there was true honor among you Astrians."

"Lady, if ever I leave this sick bed, I will right many of the wrongs your people suffered."

"Lords Carne and Drave fight for that as we speak." She knew in her heart that bad news would have filtered up to the sick room.

"My fellow auditors." He sighed. "You were with them when they rescued me from Merridale, were you not?"

"I was."

"Why?"

She paused. "They had need of my skills and you have need of a wash. You have been fevered for days." She took up the cloth and bathed his face. She wrung the cloth out, then washed his chest.

"Lady, is this seemly?"

The very words he'd spoken by Rache's pool! Adriana's heart stilled a moment. Dear Goddess! How much she had stolen from him—and herself. "Sir, I have tended you the past several days. I mean no disrespect."

"I had thought disrespect to you, lady."

"You mean none, sir. There is none."

He permitted her to wash his arms and chest, even rolling on his side to let her bathe his broad back with Rache's warm water. He still bore faint marks from the beating. After she dried his back, she spread soothing salve on his marks.

He rolled back, grasping her hand and looking up at her. "I feel my past is bound up with you, lady. Something was between us. Was it more that just saving my life?" He laughed. It was weak and tired, but was still a laugh. "How can I say 'just' to as great a service as saving my life?" He kissed her fingertips. "Lady, if you could just work the miracle to fill the voids in my mind, I would revere you the rest of my days."

Her splayed hand rested on his chest, a fingertip brushing his pink-brown nipple. She glanced down at the covers, and as she watched, the woven blanket tented over his groin.

Ignoring his erection—for now—she stroked his chest, brushing her fingertips over his nipples until they hardened and stood proud. His sharp intake of breath made her question. Was this right? Was he too weak? Not if his upright cock was any indication! It was her chance—mayhap her only one. Once he was completely recovered, he would return to his duties, but for now he was hers.

She dropped a kiss on his forehead before pulling the bedclothes lower and washing his belly and drying his skin with soft linen.

His erection was even more apparent, but she vowed not to let him be shamed by his body's evidence of his desire. And hers—for the sight of the hard flesh straining against the bedclothes aroused her.

She was tempted to strip the covers away and feast her eyes on his wondrous cock. But on reflection, she recovered his beautiful chest and raised the blankets off the bottom of the bed.

Seating herself at the foot of his pallet, she washed his feet. They were callused and still carried a few scabs, but compared to poor little Pait's, Mark's feet were beautiful and almost unmarred. She washed and dried them, and bending over, brushed a soft kiss across his toes.

"Lady!" Mark cried.

"Sir, have you not heard of healing kisses?" She smiled at his mixed shock and obvious pleasure, and kissed his other foot.

He did not protest further as she washed his shins and calves and rubbed a good quantity of salve into his grazed knees. Was he too injured to fuck? No, not by his body's evidence and, this time, he would lie back while she pleasured him—and herself—utterly.

She crossed back to the fire, warmed her basin of now-cooling water and washed his thighs. His muscles were softened from days of sickness but would soon firm up with riding and... She turned her face away as she remembered his thighs straddling her as they made love. She washed him, easing the covers upward, so they were bunched over his crotch—almost, but not quite—hiding his erection. With a little smile she drew them completely off and dropped them on the flagstones.

Mark of Windhaw gasped, raising his head and shoulders off the pillow. But he did not protest. The only sound he gave was a sigh as she washed his cock, lifting it to stroke his balls with the cloth.

"Lady," he whispered on an exhaled breath. "I know you not, but I know your touch. Your fingers are like petals on my skin. My desire should shame me, but..."

"No! No shame between us!" She set the cloth back in the basin. "Remember my promise of a healing kiss?" Before he could reply, she bent her head and covered his cock with her lips. She heard his groan and a whispered, "Sweet memories!" and swallowed him deep. She closed her eyes to concentrate on the touch of his hard warm flesh on her tongue and the taste of sweetness from his body. She eased her mouth up and down his cock and reveled in the power between her lips. Her heart seemed to swell, filling her chest. She was his as surely as she was Rache's and no longer was revenge her goal, but love.

His fingertips stroked her hair and her mind flooded with memories of the joy of their earlier coupling. If only she could share those memories with him.

She lifted her mouth, looking into his eyes, searching for some light of recognition, some flickering of remembrance. There was none.

Yet.

"Mark of Windhaw, you are mine," she whispered as she straddled him and eased herself down on his cock.

Chapter Nine

Mark stared as if transfixed—or was it astounded?—at her claim. What matter when his cock filled her warmth and her heart sang at the joy of his power within her. Smiling, she lifted herself up and down. Up to the head of his sweet cock before lowering herself to take him deep. She sighed. He groaned. He reached out with his hands, placing them on her waist, holding her steady as she moved. His hips rocked, gently at first, before picking up the rhythm and moving with her.

A light flickered in his blue eyes. She leaned forward, brushing the hair off his face and kissing his forehead, the bridge of his nose, his eyelids and his lips. As their mouths met, his lips opened and she welcomed his tongue, rubbing her herself against his chest and pressing into his body. Adriana wished she were naked too, but even more she knew she could not break this joining to strip off her clothes. Their futures depended on this physical union, on her power and his need, and the rekindling of the once-blossomed love she'd shattered.

Now she would offer her soul, her heart and her love, and strive to recreate the link between them. Her hips rocked back and forth, stroking his cock against her moist flesh and brushing her most sensitive spot against the hard bone above his cock.

His groans came louder as his need and passion peaked. She rode on and on as her desire rose. Hands now joined, they meshed fingers as she drew his passion to the heights. They were both gasping now. Adriana threw back her head and willed all power, all love and all her soul to Mark of Windhaw.

With a great shout, he came, his warmth flooding her as her heart snagged and caught before soaring with her mind. Mark cried out again and again. His eyes met hers and he screamed aloud, "Adriana! You are mine!"

She was! Utterly and completely! With heart and soul and mind! "Yes, my love," she gasped, as she leaned forward on his sweet body. "Forever, if you so will."

She felt his cock soften and ease out of her as she shifted to lie beside him.

"I love you, Adriana," he said. "I lost you in the mists of my mind, but now I have found you again. Never leave me."

"Never," she promised and kissed him. She pulled up the covers and stayed by his side until he slept.

CR SO

It was not until she stood up and straightened the covers that she realized dawn had broken and the clear light of morning flooded the room.

While Mark slept, she washed, cleaned and tidied the room, stoked the fire and demanded more than broth from the kitchen. "He is recovering now," she said. "He needs more than soup." But when she returned to the room, her arms full of stew, bread and fruit, he was gone.

Her mind whirled. Was he dead? Carried away to lie in the stone chapel? Impossible!

She set the pot of stew by the fire, the fruit and bread on the small table, and looked around. The bed was neatened, his tunic, breeches and boots missing. Had he left? Why? Surely not after saying he remembered and loved her?

She spun around at a sound in the doorway.

Mark of Windhaw stood watching her.

She stood, trying to read the expression on his face. Was it hope? Worry? No!

Love sparkled in his blue eyes.

She raced across the room and flung her arms around him and lifted her face for his kiss. It was long, hard and branding and she gloried in his possession.

"Dear heart, Adriana," he whispered against her mouth as she broke the kiss. "I pined for you and now I have found you. I should never have left you behind in the forest."

"But by staying, I found Pait and learned of the treachery against you. And I met your fellow auditors. Without them, I could never have rescued you."

"True. But now you are mine and will stay with me."

"Yes," she replied. "Without you, my soul was bereft."

"Mine, too. My mind was not my own, but you came and restored us both."

"There is much I have to tell you about that."

"Later. This afternoon, I must leave to present my report to the emperor." So soon, but it was his duty. She understood duty. She would not weep until he left. "You will come with me?"

She only half-understood his question. "Go with you?"

"To Astria, three days' ride from here. Now I am cured. I must go."

124

She smiled up at him. "To the emperor?" She would cross the fabled deserts with Mark of Windhaw by her side. "I will come."

CR ಬಿ

So Mark of Windhaw and Adriana the priestess of Rache were married that day in the stone chapel of Fort Dalban. Together they rode to the emperor and together they returned. Mark bore the emperor's commission to complete the audit, to establish justice across the conquered territories and to stamp out oppression. With the emperor's edict, Mark of Windhaw and Lady Adriana established a university where old and new lore were studied and the traditions of both Astrians and Baremes passed on. As years passed, Adriana bore Mark four sons and four daughters, and after each birth, they traveled together deep into the forest to the shrine of Rache. Each child was bathed in the warm springs and dedicated to the sweetest revenge of all—tolerance and love.

About the Author

To learn more about Rosemary Laurey, please visit www.rosemarylaurey.com.

Look for these titles by *Rosemary Laurey*

Now Available:

Country Pleasures

Paradox I
(Titled Paradox I in digital, titled Sacrifice in print)

Paradox III
(Titled Paradox III in digital, titled Stone Heart in print)

Nova

J.C. Wilder

Dedication

For Anita—You continue to amaze me, friend.

Chapter One

After this game she would be set for life.

No more lying, cheating or stealing to ensure her belly remained full, to keep clothes on her back or to provide for a roof over her head. No more picking pockets to buy a bed for the night that was free of groping hands and liquor-soaked male breath. Best of all, no more dealing with men on their terms. From here on, she would be in charge of her own destiny.

Nova shuffled her cards into an orderly pile on the table. Her coins, most of them gold, were lined in neat stacks before her. Her winnings had steadily increased, with few exceptions, while her partners' had shrunk. Her gaze assessed the money piled in the center of the table. This win, along with her cache in its hiding place near her home, would keep her for the rest of her life if she lived modestly. Never again would she have to whore her psyche for money.

But first she had to win the hand.

"You don't have a thing, Bran." Ginder, a wealthy merchant from Wryven, taunted the man across from him. "I'll see your bet of ten deuces and I raise you five." He puffed on a fat cigar as he tossed the required coins onto the pile.

The clink of gold grated across Nova's nerves, setting her even further on edge. She ran her finger along the top of her cards. This time everything would work out—it had to.

She reached for the fragrant glass of Shera, a non-alcoholic drink from the mountains in the west. The thick smoke from Ginder's cigar was making her queasy. One would think, after inhaling smoke almost every evening for the past year, it wouldn't have had any effect on her, but tonight she was in danger of gagging from the pungent fumes. Too many bad memories were associated with cigar smoke and the smell of cheap Climerian ale. She inhaled the sweet vanilla-scented fumes from her glass as she took a drink.

"And I think you're bluffing, Master Merchant," Bran replied.

Nova's gaze slid over Bran's handsome face, noting his flushed cheeks. Whether it was the effects of the wine or the agile hands of the beautiful half-naked prostitute in his lap, either one could spell disaster for Bran in a game with stakes as high as these. More money sat heaped on their gaming table than most moderately wealthy families would earn in a year.

"I'll see your bet and raise you three more." Bran tossed his coins onto the pile with a careless gesture.

She and Bran had known each other casually for several seasons. She'd judged him to be trustworthy—at least as much as a man could be trusted—and an excellent card player until he allowed his abundant alcohol consumption to cloud his judgment.

"Indeed." Ginder studied his cards with the dedicated attention of a priest at mass as he carefully fanned them out, then made minute adjustments to line up the edges. It was the faint twitch in the corner of his eye that told Nova that Bran had been right. Ginder was bluffing.

Willing herself to remain calm, she fanned her own cards to view her winning hand. Her palms grew slick and her heart thudded in her chest so hard she feared they'd be able to detect the frantic beat. Feigning a coolness she did not feel, she took another sip of her drink, hoping it wouldn't choke her.

"I'm afraid I don't have the money to stay in the game." Evi, a slim young man with once-bulging pockets, sat across from Nova. With his red hair, narrow features and shifty gaze, he resembled a fox. He'd been a late addition to the game when one of Bran's friends had failed to show. She'd had serious misgivings about him from the moment he'd entered the room. There was something about Evi that told her not to turn her back on him. The others had harbored no such feelings as they'd been distracted by the size of his purse.

In her mind, anyone who walked around with that much gold on their person deserved to be relieved of a goodly portion of it—and she was just the person to do it.

"I'm afraid all I have left is seven gold deuces and a male servant." Evi shrugged his narrow shoulders beneath a tailored white silk shirt. Even though they'd been playing for almost eight hours, the man still looked refined and elegant in a bookish sort of way. "If you'll allow me, I'd like to use him as part of my wager."

Bran laid his cards face down on the table. "You wish to wager a person?" His tone was bland, though Nova wasn't fooled. He was furious.

"A servant," Evi said. "Trust me, he's a willing participant in this matter."

"Do you engage in this behavior often?" The faint flutter of Bran's cards told her he was nervous about this hand.

"Well, not often—"

"A servant? What would I need with another servant?" Ginder laughed as he indicated the three well-dressed young men lined up behind him. They'd attended to his every need, from lighting his cigars to supplying him with ample quantities of food and drink during their long game. "I have another ten just like these at home."

Nova's gaze centered on Evi and her skin crawled. When a man was wagered in a card game, it was a good guess he was a slave. Servants were paid employees while slaves were considered possessions, chattel. This man had to be a slave if Evi was going to use him in a bid. She'd never heard of a servant who would willingly allow their employer to abuse them in such a fashion.

She forced her expression to remain impassive and reshuffled her cards as if the conversation were of no concern to her. She knew well the bonds of slavery and could not, in good conscience, allow this man to remain in Evi's possession.

"I've no problem with allowing Master Evi to place his servant on the pile." She gave a languid wave toward the money in the middle of the table. "I could always use more help around the house."

She had to bite the inside of her cheek to keep from laughing. Big lies had crossed her lips on numerous occasions; however, this one was one of the biggest. She barely had a house, let alone servants, but these men wouldn't know that. After she'd won this hand, she'd take him to her home, hire him to help fix up the house and then send him on his way with a full belly, a new set of clothing and a few coins to aid his journey. It was the least she could do to relieve a fellow victim of the hard times.

Evi straightened and for the first time his gaze veered from her bosom to her face. "Thank you, Mistress Nova. Kelwyn has been an exemplary servant for some time and, should I lose, he will make a loyal servant to you as well." His earnest expression and passionate speech gave him away. Unlike the others, he held something of value in his cards.

Ginder cast a leering glance at her breasts while his hand crept across the table toward her. "You seek a man, Nova?"

She pretended not to notice his behavior as she added her coins to the pile. "Indeed I do not." Silently, she cursed her exposed shoulders and enhanced bosom thanks to her corset. Exaggerating her feminine charms was a surefire way to distract male card players, and a distracted player was a sloppy player. But that didn't mean she had to like it.

A few seconds later, she felt Ginder's hand grope her thigh. Resisting the urge to spit in his face, she slid her bodice knife from its sheath between her breasts with a practiced flick of her wrist. She pointed it at his throat and her gaze impaled his. "Kindly remove your hand from my leg, Master Ginder." She gave him a cold hard smile. "I'd like to keep our game friendly and your blood off my winnings."

Bran laughed while Evi's eyes threatened to pop out of his head. His gaze was fixed on the unwavering steel blade a hair's breadth from Ginder's throat. Nova waggled the blade when Ginder's hand tightened on her thigh.

"Woman, I was only pretending." He released her, then straightened to move away from the lethal tip. "Why does your kind always overreact?" With shaky hands, he picked up his cards and began to shuffle them.

Bran tossed back the remains of his drink. "She's got you, Master Ginder." He set the squat glass on the table with a broad grin.

"Shut up, fool," the merchant snarled.

Nova slid her knife back into the removable sheath built into her corset. The slim handle created a delicate jeweled decoration against the plain black velvet bodice of her corset cover. Looking at it, no one would be able to tell it was a weapon, which was exactly why she'd purchased it last year at a market in Malian. At all times she kept it close at hand and this evening was no exception.

"Gentleman, I call," she said. "Lay them on the table."

Bran dropped his cards in a haphazard fan before turning his attention to the woman in his lap. Nova ran her experienced gaze over his hand. One low pair and one goddess, his hand was not even close to being a winner.

One down, two to go.

Ginder grunted his displeasure and tossed his cards onto the table. She scanned them. Nothing. Not even a master card or a lowly pair of twos. She dug her nails into her palm in an effort to contain her excitement.

One more...

Evi clutched his cards in both hands, his gaze glued to the losing hands of the other men. He licked his lips then gave a triumphant bark of laughter as his gaze met hers.

"I believe I win. One pair, two masters." He laid his cards on the table with a flourish and, for a second, Nova couldn't breathe. Her gaze skipped over the cards, once, twice, not quite believing what she saw.

"Aren't I destined to be lucky this evening?" He leaned forward to rake in his winnings when Bran grabbed his arm.

"I believe Mistress Nova has yet to show us her cards. Are you so sure you've won, friend?" His voice held a note of warning.

All three men turned toward her, their gazes riveted on the cards she held close to her chest. With her heart in her throat, she lowered the cards to the table and spread them so everyone could see the two pairs, the two master cards and the goddess she held.

She'd done it. She'd won.

Nova could barely breathe. Her senses were so focused on the cards she scarcely heard Bran give a snort of laughter, though she did feel the congratulatory slap on her shoulder that threatened to knock her off the chair. She looked up in time to see Ginder's envious glare before he turned away and muttered something uncomplimentary.

Only Evi was silent. He'd shrunk into his chair and looked miserable, horrified and defeated at the same time. The way his gaze shifted about the room, she had no doubt he'd have taken her winnings and run if he'd thought he could get away with it.

Taking a deep breath to steady herself, she twisted in her chair to retrieve the leather bag that served as her tote. "Gentlemen, I'd like to thank you for the masterful game." She opened the bag and pulled out a silk scarf that she laid across the table. She stood and began transferring her winnings into the center of the scarf. "This has been a most enjoyable and profitable evening."

Ginder grabbed her forearm, causing her to drop a few coins. "You won't even give us a chance to win back our losses?" he demanded.

"Not this evening." Nova nodded toward a partially opened window. The sky was still dark, but soon the eastern sky would herald the coming of the sun. "It's late and I'm very tired."

"But you must give us a chance to regain our losses." Evi's tone was strident and he leaned toward her, desperation written on his face.

She glanced out the window again. Time was wasting and, while she had no intention of playing cards with these men again, it might do well to fool these men into thinking she'd return tomorrow.

She met his gaze with what she hoped was an inviting smile. "If you insist, Master Evi. Please meet me here this evening one hour after sundown. We'll resume our seats and see who is the best strategist for a second night."

She dumped the rest of her winnings into the scarf and tied the ends into a bundle. Bran probably had an inkling of her plans, but he'd never give her away. She shoved the bundle into her tote and slung it over her shoulder. The weight of her winnings threatened to break the worn leather strap. Lucky for her she didn't have to walk very far.

"Now Master Evi, if you'll be so kind as to direct me toward my new servant, I will be on my way to bed." She caught the look of irritation that flashed across his face before he masked it with a cool smile. Yes, she would be well served to keep her eye on this one.

"As you wish." He rose from his chair, taking care to brush the wrinkles from his tailored pants before retrieving his cape from the hook by the door. "If you'll follow me, mistress."

Nova nudged Bran's arm, dragging his attention away from the prostitute's ample bosom. "Will you accompany me, Master Bran?"

He nodded, then whispered something to the young woman in his lap. She giggled and stood, allowing him to rise.

Nova retrieved her cloak and gave Ginder a parting nod that he returned with great reluctance. Guess they weren't parting friends. She quashed a grin as she turned and followed Evi from the room.

The private game room they'd left was situated in the back of the Laughing Gryphon Gaming Salon. The secluded location of the private rooms ensured maximum privacy and anonymity for the high stakes players. There were several exits that would enable someone to escape unnoticed by the patrons of the establishment in the main salon.

Evi led them through one of the larger gaming rooms and Nova wasn't surprised to see it devoid of players at this late—or very early—hour. Three women wielded brooms on the expanse of polished floor while several men were perched on ladders to clean the glittering chandeliers. A variety of game tables were arranged around the room and all were tidy. The chairs for the patrons were turned upside down on the tables to make the sweeping easier.

The bartenders were polishing glasses behind the bar while the cashiers counted the day's take, safe in their wrought iron cages at each end of the room. Judging from the upscale furnishings, the Laughing Gryphon appeared to do a good business.

When they approached the entrance, a beautiful attendant resplendent in black and red silk opened the door. With Bran bringing up the rear, the threesome exited into the cool, crisp morning. Overhead the stars were bright and Nova took a deep breath, eager to rid herself of the stench of cigars and booze. They walked down the wide front steps and Bran grabbed one of the brass torches to light their way.

She pulled her cloak over her shoulders against the cold air. After securing the closure, she checked to ensure she could reach her knife with ease. She had a small fortune tucked into her tote and had no intention of losing it now.

Evi led them to the south end of the building to a gravel lot in front of the stables. A neat row of coaches was beside the stable and on the far end was a peddler wagon that looked out of place among the expensive conveyances. It was painted dark gray and the closed compartment on the back was tall enough for a man to stand in. There were no markings to indicate a traveling merchant used it. How curious.

Their guide led them around the back of the wagon to a narrow door. Her eyes widened at the sight of the numerous locks and chains that held it shut. The door and the molding around it was a lighter color than the rest of the wagon, indicating it had been recently replaced.

"Mistress Nova," Evi spoke. "Since we'll be playing again tomorrow evening maybe it's better if I keep him with me until—"

"That won't be necessary." Nova nodded toward the locks. "If you'll open the door, please."

His thin lips tightened and he withdrew a ring of keys from his pocket. As he did so, two men exited the stables and headed in their direction. Nova could feel Bran tensing with each step they took.

"Boss?" The tall blond one gave a wide yawn.

"Open the door, Ber." Evi threw the keys at his chest, forcing the man to step back in order to catch them. "Dreg," he spoke to the second man, "get ready."

Nova glanced at Bran's expressionless face. Only his eyes were alive and alert as they moved from man to man, assessing them, as the blond unlocked the door. After the blond removed the last chain, he let it slide to the ground in a rattle of iron against iron. The door swung open and Bran hoisted the torch higher to illuminate the interior.

The floor of the wagon was littered with dirty straw, and the stench of human waste and rotted food was overpowering. Against the back wall stood a man clad in filthy rags and dirt. He was quite tall, his head stooped to avoid hitting the roof. His dirty, tangled hair obscured most of his face with the exception of his eyes. Hatred burned hot in their glittering depths. If looks could wound, Nova knew she'd be dead where she stood. His lip curled when his gaze settled on Evi and he emitted a low growl.

The one called Ber climbed into the wagon and the so-called servant moved forward in an aggressive lunge, stopped short by the thick chains that tethered his wrists to the wagon wall. His ankles were cuffed as well, the chain so short he'd be unable to walk far even if he were to get free.

"This is what you call a servant?" Nova spat.

"Yes, Kelwyn has served us well." Evi smirked; his gaze was fixed on the chained man.

Evi enjoyed this man's humiliation. Nova's stomach churned. There was nothing she despised more than slavery. She'd spent almost six years as a slave before she'd managed to buy her freedom just over a year ago. Still, she had nightmares of the degradation she'd been forced to endure during her time of captivity.

"Do you treat all of your servants as such?" Her tone was flat.

"Kelwyn must be beaten to obey my commands," Evi shot back.

"Release him."

"No."

Dreg tossed Ber a short wooden club that had been hanging on a hook near the door. Ber advanced toward the chained man, the club held in a striking posture. Kelwyn's stance didn't alter; he continued to lean against the chains, pulling at them with all his might. Beneath the dirt and rags, muscles bulged with the strain.

"You'll need to keep him chained—" Evi was saying.

Ber moved closer, the club held higher. If he swung at Kelwyn...

"I said release him." Nova's voice was hard, unflinching. "You put him on the table and you lost. He's no longer your responsibility, Master Evi, he's mine."

"Mistress—"

The sound of wood striking flesh caused her to look in time to see Ber raise the club for another strike. Putting aside any thoughts of self-preservation, she leapt into the wagon and darted between the two combatants. The club whooshed through the air and narrowly missed hitting her shoulder. Whipping out her blade, she pointed it at Ber's nose.

"Back off or you'll be breathing through a hole in the center of your face," she snarled. Behind her, she felt Kelwyn standing close. The stench of his unwashed body was so overpowering that her eyes were beginning to water and she imagined she could feel his hot breath on the back of her neck.

Ber glanced at Evi and out of the corner of her eye Nova caught his imperceptible nod. Ber moved away and, as he did so, lowered the club. The message in his eyes promised retribution for both her and the man she protected. Satisfied the threat had passed, Nova headed for the door.

"Release him," she spoke to Evi. "I will secure—"

A snarl and a thud had her swinging around in time to see Kelwyn fall to the filthy straw, a victim of a single blow to the head. He lay motionless, his arm outstretched as if to seek her help.

Rage flared and without a second thought, Nova felled Ber with a sharp kick to the side of his knee. With a sickening crunch and a scream of pain, the man went down hard, narrowly missing the overflowing slop jar. Still screaming, he rolled on the floor, clutching his knee.

"You broke me fuckin' leg!" he howled.

"No, but by tomorrow you'll wish it was broken." She stepped over the writhing man. Eschewing the steps to leap to the ground, she forced Evi to step back a few feet. "Get out of my sight," she snarled at him. She replaced the knife and picked up the keys where they sat on the top step and flung them at the one called Dreg. "Release him immediately."

"Miss—" Evi spoke.

Bran placed himself between them. "Now, runt." His tone was mild, but Nova could tell he wanted Evi to make a move against him.

Frustrated yet defeated for the moment, Evi shot her a hot glance before he turned on his heel and stalked toward the main doors.

"He'll be back." Bran didn't sound as if he minded going for another round.

"Indeed he will." She headed toward the stables. "Make sure this one gets Kelwyn unlocked while I retrieve my cart. I want to get out of this godforsaken place before the sun comes up."

"Aye."

The short walk cooled her temper and she was marginally calmer when she entered the relative peace of the stable. It took only a few moments to locate the stable master from whom she'd purchased a small hay cart and a mare the night before. After giving him instructions to bring it around front as soon as possible, she returned to the peddler's wagon.

Bran was inside, crouched by the unconscious man. Everyone else had gone.

"He feels warm," he said.

"Fever?"

"Could be." He wiped his hand on his pants as he stood. "Whatever it is, you'll want to take care with it. You don't want him dying on you."

The clop of hooves and the rattle of her cart heralded the arrival of the stable master.

"Here y'ar, mistress." He dropped the lead rope over the wheel of the peddler's wagon, then peered inside. "Whatcha got in dere?"

"A man in need of help. Can you secure me blankets, a cloak and some food and ale?" She removed a gold coin from her cloak pocket and held it up so that the man could see it. She was well aware she was offering him more money than he'd probably earn in a fortnight. The better the pay, the better the service, was her opinion.

His eyes widened and he bobbed his head. "Y-y-yes miss, right 'way." He handed her his lantern and rushed away to do her bidding.

Bran eased the unconscious man onto his back. "This Kelwyn is a big guy," he said.

"Indeed." Nova set down the lantern and climbed into the wagon.

He was tall, at least several inches taller than she, and was broadly built. Even though it was obvious he'd been sorely misused, he looked strong. His upper body was corded with a thick layer of muscles, though he wasn't a bulging brute like a soldier or a blacksmith. She crouched beside him and pushed a tattered section of his shirt aside to reveal the abraded skin stretched across his ribs. Judging from the marks on his body, he'd been treated badly for several months at least. Some of the bruises and whip marks were old while others were still fresh. But with a few weeks of good meals and ample rest, this man would be back in fighting form.

Bran cursed beneath his breath as she covered him up again. "What are you going to do with him?"

"Clean him up, hire him for some work around my home, then grant him his freedom." She rose. "I could use an extra pair of hands for a few weeks."

He shook his head. "You watch yourself, Nova. You know nothing about this man or his character. Judging from his earlier behavior, he could be dangerous."

She couldn't help but laugh and she nudged him with her elbow. "You're a fine one to talk. I knew nothing about your character either, but that didn't stop me from pulling you out of a trough when that innkeeper in Lanaise tried to drown you."

"And I'll wager you've regretted it a time or two since." He smiled at the memory.

"That's an understatement."

Bran was probably the only person in the world she would even think to call a friend. Their paths had crossed frequently as they'd traveled all over the country. With their common goals of gambling and amassing their fortunes, they'd made a good pair, though she'd always suspected he'd come from money to begin with. Being born into a moneyed family always left a mark like brown hair or green eyes.

"Shall we get your new hired hand out of here?"

She wrinkled her nose at their fragrant surroundings. "Yes, please."

Taking note of Kelwyn's deep abrasions from the iron cuffs that now lay on the floor, she grabbed one hand while Bran took the other. As they pulled him toward the door, she couldn't help but notice his skin was very warm and his fingers were callused. Obviously he was a man who'd been used to physical labor before being caged like an animal.

When they reached the door, Nova leapt out and took several deep breaths of the sweet fresh air, willing the stench away. The scent of human waste and rotted food always brought back memories of her own enslavement. She shook away her dark thoughts to maneuver the cart closer to the door of the wagon. Together they lifted him, with Bran supporting most of his weight, and transported him the few feet into the clean hay in the back of her cart. Once he was settled, she offered her thanks to Bran.

"You've done me a great service, my friend," she said. "You know where to find me?"

"Indeed I do." Bran tweaked her braid. "Be mindful of your surroundings, Nova. Perhaps I will see you soon."

"And you, my friend, be mindful as well."

He retrieved his torch and, with a wave, headed for the front entrance of the gaming hall as the stable master returned out of breath. He carried a pile of blankets as well as a heavy black cloak. Behind him were two sleepy-eyed kitchen girls, each bearing overflowing baskets of provisions.

Taking charge of the blankets, Nova and the women carefully bundled the unconscious man before placing the cloak over the top. While she hated putting clean blankets against his filthy body, she had no choice in the matter. Once he was up and about he'd be able to wash himself and they could burn the blanket lying closest to his skin. After seeing to his comfort and stowing the baskets, she showed her appreciation by giving the girls a few extra silver coins.

Thanks to the addition of her new companion, her journey would be lengthened by at least a day, but that couldn't be helped. Until she was sure of his physical condition, she'd have to take rest breaks every couple of hours or so just to see to his comfort.

She looked at Kelwyn, unconscious in his slumber. She couldn't bear the thought of leaving him in this condition and in the hands of a master such as Evi. She shuddered. While enslaved, the number of times she'd wished someone would rescue her were countless. In the end, she'd had to rescue herself.

Besides, she could afford an extra day on the road. It wasn't as if anyone or anything awaited her at the end of her journey. Just an empty wreck of a house and a hidden bag of gold coins and neither would object to her late arrival.

Climbing onto the narrow seat, she picked up the reins and gave them a jiggle. As the first rays of sunlight kissed the horizon, the cart moved forward with a jerk.

Nova was going home.

Chapter Two

Consciousness slammed into his skull with the delicacy of a hammer.

Wyn sat up so fast he thought his head would explode. Stifling a groan, he gripped the side of the cart and eased back into the hay. Bile burned his throat and he concentrated on not throwing up or passing out. After a few moments, the nausea receded and he dared to open his eyes.

Angry gray clouds churned overhead, allowing only a few tiny beams of sunlight to slip through. Amazed that he could even see the sky above, he took a deep breath, filling his lungs with fresh air. He wanted to weep at the sweetness of its scent. It had been so long since he'd breathed something other than filth and decay that he couldn't get enough of its clean bouquet. He gulped in air until his head buzzed and he was sure this wasn't a dream.

Slower this time, he levered himself upright, alert to any signs of the pain and nausea that had assailed him only minutes before. Satisfied he wouldn't pass out, he raised his hand to his face only to realize he was no longer chained. Shocked, he stared at his damaged wrists where the iron cuffs had rubbed them raw. Scabs were already forming over the injuries and they looked sore and angry. He inspected his other wrist to see it was in the same condition. All he needed was several days in the sea and he'd be fully healed.

He frowned. What had transpired to convince Evi to give him up?

Images flashed through his mind. The door opening, people standing outside, peering in at him, one holding a torch high to ensure a good look. And then the rage. The fury that had swept through him when he saw Evi standing next to the beautiful dark-haired woman had almost brought him to his knees.

He rubbed his forehead where it felt like it would split in two. He'd never seen her before, he was sure of it. Who was she and why had she been with a monster like Evi? Was she one of his kind? A slaver?

The wagon hit something in the road, causing pain to ricochet through his skull, and he gritted his teeth against the resulting wave of nausea. He closed his eyes and willed his stomach to settle.

Gathering strength, he turned his head until he saw the slim figure on the wagon seat above. Concealed in a bulky cloak with the hood pulled up, he couldn't tell if it was a man or woman. He caught the distinctive tang of Alyrian pipe tobacco, which probably meant the driver was a man. Who'd ever heard of a woman smoking a pipe? Whoever he was, he wasn't very big and it would only take a matter of seconds to overtake him... When Wyn got the energy to do so, that is.

With his head aching, he pulled the blankets up to his shoulders and burrowed into the warmth of his cocoon. For now, he was more than content to enjoy the brief luxury of clean hay and fresh air. There would be time enough to find out how he'd ended up in the back of this little cart rather than chained in the wagon.

For now he could just...be.

Wyn pulled his right arm from beneath the blankets and grimaced when he saw the layer of dirt and dried blood that coated his skin. His nails were blackened with grime and his knuckles were battered. Spreading his fingers, he examined the thin, gossamer skin that webbed his hand from the first knuckle down to his palm. Barely noticeable to the human eye, the webbing served no purpose on land, though in the sea it enabled his kind to move like lightning across the sky.

His fist clenched and he let his arm drop to his side. This webbing and that between his toes had marked him as different from humans. It, along with his own stupidity, had resulted in his capture and subsequent enslavement a year ago.

But now he was free, or away from his tormentors at least.

He closed his eyes. He knew he should get up, overpower his driver and steal off with the cart, but he didn't have the energy to do so. The comforting rocking sensation of the wagon—when they weren't hitting the bumps, that is—combined with the rich scent of pipe smoke and freshly baked bread...

Bread?

His stomach gave a loud growl and he shot a look up at the driver. If he'd heard, he gave no indication as neither his position nor his speed changed. Releasing a pent-up breath, Wyn looked under the shelf created by the wagon seat. There were two baskets and a large leather satchel secured there. Propping himself on one elbow, he pushed back the cloth covering the nearest basket and a myriad of tantalizing scents rose from its depths. If his nose didn't deceive him, it was filled with food and a goodly amount at that.

Keeping his gaze glued on the driver's back, he pawed through the basket until he came to a wedge of something he thought was cheese and a hunk of coarse brown bread.

Desperately hungry, he stuffed the food into his mouth as quickly as he could. The nutty flavor of the bread blended with the sharp tang of the cheddar and he wanted to sing with happiness. Never had such simple fare tasted so good.

After he had finished his snack, he reached in again and located a large chunk of cooked sausage wrapped in greasy paper. He bit into it and the combined flavors of pork and sage burst across his tongue. Chewing as fast as he could, he devoured the hunk of meat.

When he finished, he rummaged once more until he pulled out something soft that was wrapped in thin waxy paper. He unwrapped it and held it to his nose. Pastry? He bit into it and this time he did groan as the flavor of ripe raspberries exploded in his mouth. The flaky tart was plump with fruit and walnuts and liberally sweetened with honey. He polished off the pastry and longed to lick his fingers clean, but stopped himself at the last second, remembering their filthy state. He opted to wipe his hands on his equally dirty shirt—or what was left of it.

Replete for the first time in many moon cycles, Wyn was content. He curled up in his hay and blanket cocoon and closed his eyes. When the wagon stopped, he would assert his will over the driver, but until then his full belly was making him sleepy.

Finally, his luck had changed.

ଓ ଞ

Nova couldn't prevent a grin when she heard the soft snore from the bed of the cart. She'd known her companion had been awake for the past hour or so but she'd opted to say nothing. Instead she'd pulled out her pipe and lit it, preferring to enjoy a smoke as she'd waited for him to make the first move. He'd surprised her. Judging from his earlier aggression, she'd thought for sure he'd make his presence known immediately. Instead he'd opted to gorge himself and go back to sleep.

Typical.

A rumble of thunder turned her attention to the clouds that roiled overhead. They'd grown angrier with each passing hour. The sun had risen many hours before, but rather than getting brighter as the day had progressed, it had grown darker with the approaching storm. Time for the nooning meal had long since passed and the wind was picking up from the west, the breeze thick with the scent of coming rain. Inclement weather or not, it wasn't time to stop for a break, especially since she knew they were being followed.

She took a final drag on her pipe. There was no doubt in her mind that it was Evi or his men. Seeing that there were only two of them on horseback, she'd guess it was his men as Evi had been quite put out at losing. She grimaced. The man was a fool. The first rule of gambling was to never bet more than one could stand to lose. She'd learned that the hard way. It was obvious to her that he hadn't wanted to lose this so-called servant of his. No doubt he thought he could reclaim him with little struggle from her.

He was sadly mistaken.

Nova tapped out the dying embers from her pipe before stowing it in her pocket. As she did so, she glanced over her shoulder at the long bumpy road they'd just covered. In the distance, she could see the two riders. They traveled at a pace to match hers and didn't appear to be in any hurry to overtake her. The hairs on the back of her neck prickled. Considering a horse alone was much faster than her little cart, their behavior was suspicious.

She faced forward and gave the reins a jiggle, causing the brown mare to pick up her pace. Ahead the road stretched flat and wide for another mile or so and beyond that the woods closed in. In the stretch of dense trees and undergrowth, losing her unwanted companions would be no problem. There were numerous paths branching off the main one and it would be easy to slip through any of the villages and leave them far behind.

She glanced over her shoulder at the man still sleeping in the bed of the cart, though she could see little more than matted hair and the tip of his nose. "I hope you're worth the trouble," she muttered.

The last thing she wanted was to slow her journey home, but she couldn't lead these men right to her doorstep. She wouldn't be safe nor would her companion. Besides, she was determined that nothing of her former life would intrude upon the new one she was about to create.

Nothing.

Chapter Three

The first drops of rain landed on the back of Nova's hands as they reached the woods. Muttering curses strong enough to singe hair, she ducked under a low hanging branch as she urged the horse faster. Spying a large root sticking up in the middle of the road, she braced her feet beneath the footrest seconds before the wheels of the cart made contact hard enough to lift her off the seat several inches. Behind her, she heard her companion stir.

"God's teeth, do you think to kill us?" he roared.

Her grip tightened on the reins as they tore down the path. "If I'd wanted you dead, you'd be cold by now," she shouted.

"And we'll both be cold soon enough if you keep up this pace," he said.

"Criticizing me is helping so much, thanks." Her words dripped with sarcasm. "Look behind us. What do you see?"

There was a slight pause.

"Two men on horseback. Why are we being followed?"

"You would know better than I."

He muttered something unpleasant.

"My feelings exactly. So why don't you help by shutting up and letting me concentrate?" She ground her teeth in near frustration as her hood slid back and a drop of rain struck her in the eye. How was it rain managed that maneuver even when she squinted?

"Do you know where you're going?" His voice sounded close to her ear and she jerked in reaction. The man had risen to his knees and his big hands were curled over the edge of her seat. He was so close his chin could have rested on her shoulder.

"We can lose them on one of the side roads. The rain is hard enough to destroy our tracks." She ducked as a broken tree limb threatened to remove her head from her shoulders.

"Careful now."

Broad arms slid around her waist, anchoring her to both him and the seat. For a split second, she thought about grabbing her dagger and giving him what for, but decided against it when the wagon hit another bump and threw her against his muscular arm. She'd have flown off the seat if it weren't for him anchoring her. Forcing herself to relax and accept his help, she decided to concentrate on driving and deal with him later.

As they continued their headlong race through the woods, not a word was spoken. The thud of hooves and the racket of wheels punctuated their haste. Soon the deepening darkness and muddy track hampered their progress. She could barely see more than a few feet ahead of the horse's muzzle. She was forced to slow even more as the path grew muddier with every step.

Alongside the road, she caught sight of an ancient elm with a large abrasion on the north side. She knew that tree, and more importantly, what lay beyond it. She pulled hard on the reins.

"We turn here!" she shouted against the rising wind. "We're close to the ruins of an old monastery and we can bed down there for the night. We should be safe enough."

"Do you think they'll know about it?"

"I doubt it. Only the locals know it even exists and they won't venture there. It burned centuries ago and should be empty." She shot a grin over her shoulder. "It's said to be haunted."

His face was a pale oval shrouded by wet, matted hair. He grinned and white teeth flashed against the grime on his face. "Sounds like the place for us."

She tugged to the right and the horse turned onto a narrow path. It was so overgrown it looked as if no one had set foot on it for years. In several places tree limbs and overgrown brush scraped the sides of the cart and they had to duck to avoid low tree branches.

Nova released a sigh of relief when the moss-covered walls of the abbey loomed out of the darkness. She pulled the horse to a stop and, without a word, she and her traveling companion climbed out of the cart. She stretched, then groaned, as her body, cramped from the long ride, was forced into action. Bracing a stiff hand at the small of her back, she painfully approached the structure she remembered so well from childhood.

The main building of the abbey compound was a squat gray stone structure that bore scant evidence of the inferno that had killed many of the monks who'd lived there. Much to their mother's dismay, she and her sister, Dani, had found a human skull while playing in the area of the chapel. Her family had spent a quiet season here and she remembered it as one of the few peaceful times in her childhood. Only a few months later, her mother was dead and her family on the run from the Peacekeepers.

Nova stepped through an arched doorway and into what had once served as the living quarters for the monks. The west end of the building sported the only section that retained a roof and it was still intact. Several large timbers were jammed into place to brace the sagging overhead supports. No doubt an addition from visiting travelers.

The debris that had once occupied the center of the building had been cleared. The stone floor was cracked in several places and thick patches of weeds grew through the openings. She came to a halt when she found a small tree growing in the middle of what had been the dining hall.

Life did move on.

She ventured into the area covered by the narrow slice of roof. The space was dry and a mixture of hay and summer grasses covered the stone floor. The fireplace had caved in, and in the far corner, someone had constructed a fire ring with a hole in the roof directly above it for the smoke to escape. Near the ring was a pile of dry wood and tinder. No doubt the visitors who'd used the place over the years had left it behind.

There was plenty of room for them and the horse to bed down for the night. The cart would have to stay outside and the rain would ruin the hay, but there was nothing she could do about that. Hay could be replaced easily enough and she wasn't going to waste time worrying about it. Now she just had to find her companion and they could get settled—

She turned and slammed into a warm, very male chest. Startled, she jumped back to scowl up at Kelwyn.

"Don't do that," she snapped.

He stepped back and held up his hands. "Do what?"

She glared at him. "Sneak up on me like that."

He shrugged. "I'm sorry." He gave her a quick bow. "My name is Kelwyn of Rom de Mer." He lowered his hands. "You can call me Wyn."

She considered herself to be well traveled, but she'd never heard of Rom de Mer. Was it in the east somewhere? "Where's that?"

"South," he said. "What shall I call you?"

"Nova." She moved, careful to keep more than an arm's length away. "Please don't follow me like that again. I don't like it."

"I wanted to make sure you remained unaccosted."

He crossed his arms over his chest and Nova saw that she'd underestimated him. Standing fully upright, he was bigger than she'd originally thought. He towered over her by at least six inches and outweighed her by a minimum of sixty pounds. While he had obvious injuries and the skin on his wrists looked especially painful, he also looked like a man who was fit and sure of himself.

"Well, thank you, but I can take care of myself." She exited the abbey. "I need you to unhook the horse and bring her inside. She can be stabled on that side and we can bed down here near the fire ring. It's not luxurious, but it will be dry at least."

Not waiting for an answer, Nova walked to the cart, still annoyed with herself for allowing him to sneak up on her. She knew better. Another mistake like that and she could end up with a blade between her ribs.

She retrieved the basket of food, pleased to see that Wyn had bunched the blankets beneath the wagon seat so only the top one was damp. Grabbing an armload, she hauled their meager supplies into the abbey. As she passed Wyn, she heard him talking to the horse, telling her what a fine creature she was and thanking her for seeing them safely to their destination.

She rolled her eyes as she stomped her way through the ruins. What nonsense. She loved animals as much as anyone, but no one would ever catch her talking to the beasts as if they could understand. She dumped their supplies near the fire ring then returned to collect the food.

He was entering the abbey with the horse in tow as she exited. He winked at her as he passed and he was still conversing with the beast.

"We're going to bed down here and, in the morning, we'll continue. Is that all right with you?" He ran his hand down the side of the horse's neck and, to Nova's amazement, the horse nickered as if in agreement.

She shook her head. The man was crazed—he had to be. It was likely too many weeks in chains that had warped his mind. It wasn't unusual for a person to be broken by slavery, and for some slave owners, that was precisely their goal. Once a slave was broken, it was rare they tried to escape their keeper. She'd seen it many times and had barely managed to save herself from that sad fate. She hunched her shoulders against the driving rain as she hurried to retrieve her pack and the final basket. Her clothing was so damp her skin was getting chafed and she couldn't wait to get out of them.

When she returned, Wyn was rubbing the horse with handfuls of dry hay, still talking to her in low tones. Nova ignored them and headed for the corner where they were to bed down for the night. She stowed her load and set about arranging sticks and dried grasses to light a fire. She judged they were far enough from the main road to warrant a small fire, something to warm their toes at least. She knew she was near to frozen and she was wearing more clothes than he was. Unfortunately she had very little to change into save the blankets. She glanced at Wyn, who was finishing with the horse. She had nothing for him to wear either.

Blankets it was.

After she started the fire with her handy flint, she retrieved a length of cord from her pack to string a makeshift clothesline. Overnight, their clothing just might dry if she could get the line close enough to the fire. After securing the cord, she removed her sodden cloak and tossed it over the line before unbuttoning her black velvet corset cover. She couldn't wait to burn these clothes. As beautiful as the velvet was, it still represented her former life. The life she was determined to leave behind.

"Is there anything I can do?"

Nova jumped, completely unaware Wyn was near. Damn, he was quiet.

"I think we're all set. Just remove your clothes and put them over the line to dry. You can bundle in one of those for the night." She pointed at the pile of blankets. "That's all we have for now."

He stood, just looking at her, his expression confused. "Have I met you before?" His eyes widened, then narrowed. "I saw you with Evi."

"Yes?" She flung the velvet over the line. "Last night I was with him when I saw you for the first time."

His expression was dark as he turned and peered into the darkness, his body tense as if expecting someone to leap out at him.

"What's wrong?" She withdrew her knife.

"Where is he?" His voice was terse.

"Where is who?" She looked around, but could see nothing out of the ordinary, just the falling rain and darkness.

"You're too beautiful to be in this alone," he snarled. "Where is Evi? Is he following you?"

"I have no idea where that bastard is. Why are you asking about him?" She shoved the knife into its sheath. "I won you in a card game. The fool put you on the table as part of a bet and he lost. When I saw you in that wagon, I knew I couldn't leave you with him. So here we are."

She could tell from his silence that she'd shocked him. Well, he'd shocked her by almost saying she was in cahoots with Evi. Irritated, she pulled her boots off and set them by the fire.

"You won me in a card game—"

"I did." She braced her fists on her hips. "I won you with a particularly good hand of Goddess and Dragons. That said, get undressed before you catch your death. I'm not nursing you because you're intent on talking to me while you should be drying off."

His eyes were narrowed and she had the feeling this conversation wasn't over, not by a long shot. Firelight flickered over his muscular frame as he picked up a blanket. He removed his shirt, balled it up and tossed it into a corner. His back was covered with whip marks and deep bruises caused by a baline, a leather-covered steel ball tethered to a stick that, when struck against human flesh, left a deep, painful bruise. She was well familiar with both instruments of torture.

She shoved those memories away, then removed her knife and stowed it in one of her boots where she could reach it easily if needed. Tugging on the corset laces, she heaved a sigh of relief as the steel-boned garment loosened its cruel grip. She hated wearing the contraption, but it served two very important purposes. First, the steel boning acted almost as efficiently as armor and it had saved her life on at least one occasion. The second reason was that her increased bosom helped to distract men when she fleeced them as she had the previous evening.

"Does that hurt?" Wyn asked.

Nova glanced over her shoulder to find him standing near the fire, a blanket wrapped around his waist.

"The corset?" She pulled it off and held up the pale blue garment. "It isn't terribly comfortable, but it is a necessary evil by the standards of fashion."

"Why is it that?"

"Most women wear corsets nowadays." She tossed it over the line, then jerked her damp black velvet pants off.

"But you dress in pants like a man. It appears to me that you don't care much for fashion."

"Thanks." Her tone was sarcastic. Clad only in her long cotton drawers, Nova snatched up a blanket and wrapped it sarong-style around her breasts before adding the pants to the makeshift line. "We need to tend to your wounds."

He looked down at his wrists. "How bad is my back?"

"I've seen worse." She picked up her bag and moved it closer to him. "I have some salve that will help, but first we need to get you clean. You're an infection waiting to happen."

He held up his filthy hands. "How do you recommend we do that?"

She indicated the basket containing bottles of wine and water. "We have water here. And you can start by using that." She pointed toward a section of the roof where the rainwater fell in a steady steam. "Then we'll rinse your wounds with this water and I'll apply the salve."

Wyn rose and stalked toward the stream and, before she could voice an objection, he'd stripped off his blanket and stepped into the spray. Flickering firelight cast shadows over his body as he turned this way and that to wet himself. His legs turned dark as the dirt embedded in his skin changed to mud.

She shivered just watching him. It was too cold to even think about bathing, but she could see the temperature didn't appear to bother him. Maybe he was so desperate to wash the taint of slavery and humiliation from his skin that the chilly temperature was the least of his concerns.

She could understand that feeling.

She rummaged in her bag until she found bathing supplies—a slim bar of soap, a bathing cloth and a vial of liquid soap for her hair. She placed the items on a broken timber where he could reach them.

"Thank you." His tone was sincere, and for a second, Nova felt a lump in her throat.

She nodded and moved away to situate herself near the fire where she could still keep an eye on him, but also allow him privacy for his bathing. She removed first aid supplies from her pack and arranged them on a flat rock near the fire. She'd purchased clean white cloth a few days ago that she'd fashioned into rags for her monthlies. These could be used for bandages on his wrists.

"How far south is your home?" She added a few small logs to the fire. He'd need a bigger fire to get warm after the impromptu bath. She sat cross-legged, then was dismayed to realize she now had a clear view of him.

"Near the cliffs of Maragorn." He was scrubbing his hair. "Do you know the area?"

"I do." She swallowed hard as rainwater ran down his lean body. His long, wet hair clung to his skin and muscles rippled as he scrubbed. Tipping his head back, she was struck by the strength of his profile, his determined chin, his sensual mouth...

Her throat dry, she leapt to her feet and retrieved the food basket. Keeping her eyes down, she toted it closer to the fire, then sat with her back to him. She cleared her throat. "You'll be happy to know we're heading south and our final destination is close to Maragorn." She pulled a small, round loaf of bread from the basket.

"Is that where you live?"

A whisper of delight passed down her spine. Where she would live. Where she was prepared to set up roots and create a home, a real home.

"Nova?"

She started when she realized she'd neglected to answer him. "Sorry, I was thinking." She tore the bread in half. "Yes, that's where I live. I bought a house on the cliffs overlooking the sea."

Large bare feet appeared next to her on the blanket. "So you'll be letting me go?" His voice was low.

"Am I holding you now?" She looked up at him and offered him half her bread.

He hesitated, his greenish-blue gaze wary, but Nova didn't waver. Finally, he must have found what he was searching for in her face when he took her offering. He sank beside her and she noticed the gleam of water on his skin and wondered why he wasn't shivering. If it had been her, she'd be freezing.

"No, you're not holding me." He broke the bread in half.

"Well, I did win you." She smiled. "So I guess you're mine to keep."

His brow quirked. "Is that how you feel about slavery? People are possessions?"

Irritated, she shook her head. Didn't he realize she'd just saved him? "Not at all. Do you see any chains? Would someone who believed in slavery and wished to keep you in such a state remove the bonds that mark you as such?" She retrieved her knife from her boot, cut a large wedge of cheese and held it out to him on the tip of the blade.

"A smart woman would." He took the offering.

"Why is that?" She rose and grabbed the pot of salve.

"A smart woman would remove the chains to lull her slave into a false sense of security, thus binding him to her."

Nova didn't answer. He was right, but she didn't believe in the barbaric practice, and if he chose to assist her with restoring her home, he'd be a paid employee rather than a slave. At any time he'd be free to go, no questions asked.

"Yes, well, I'm not very educated so you don't have to worry about that." She picked up the long wet strands of his hair. "Now hold still while I apply this." Her fingers struck something hard and she found two narrow braids behind his left ear. Near the bottom of the braid were several small seashells.

How...exotic...

"You may not be book smart, but you're clever." Wyn wrapped bread around the cheese and took a large bite. "So once we reach our destination, I'm a free man?"

She laid his hair over his shoulder, then opened the jar of salve. Digging her fingers into the waxy, oily mixture, she spread it over the worst of his wounds. Beneath her fingers and through the cool salve, his skin was surprisingly warm and supple. How long had it been since she'd willingly gotten this close to a man?

She cleared her throat. "If that's what you wish. If you'd like to earn some money before you leave, I'd appreciate it if you could give me a hand for a few weeks or so."

He tensed beneath her hand. "In what way?"

"The home I've purchased is in sorry shape and I'll need manual labor to fix it up before I can move in." She shot a rueful glance over her shoulder at the rain falling a few feet away. "As the wet season is fast approaching, I don't have much time to secure the roof and I've no desire to wake up swimming in my bed."

"That's a sound plan." He gave her a slow nod. "Very well then, Nova. Since you live near Maragorn, which is very close to my home, in exchange for my freedom I'll be more than willing to help in setting up your house."

Finished with his back, she moved around then crouched to attend his wrists. "Thank you." She spread the thick salve over his right wrist, her movements slowing when his fingers brushed her palm. She raised her head and their gazes met. In the depths of his eyes, she saw trust, strength and she thought that maybe, just maybe, Wyn was a man who could be trusted—

Had she lost her mind? What was she thinking?

Disturbed, she released his arm and stood. "You can finish this. I'm exhausted and I'm going to turn in."

Not meeting his eyes, she shoved the salve and bandages at him before grabbing several blankets. She scurried around the fire to create her pallet on the other side. With her back toward Wyn, she stretched out and closed her eyes.

They would journey to her home, he'd help her set her house to rights and in a week or so he'd be gone. She was determined all Wyn would take with him was some new clothing, a few coins and nothing else.

Chapter Four

A tremendous crack of thunder roused Wyn from a deep sleep. Torrents of rain lashed the abbey walls and the place where he'd taken his improvised shower had turned into a wild cascade. The sound of the newly created waterfall was comforting.

It was the sound of home.

His eyes closed for a second and the pain of separation was breath-stealing. He couldn't wait to return to his family and friends. By now they probably thought him long dead, though surely they wondered what had happened to him.

He'd been on his way home after a fortnight in Mer de Luna when he'd been captured. His men would have been quick to raise the alarm, but there was little they could do. His people had very little contact with the land dwellers. Where would they have gone for help? When he returned that was one of the first things he was determined to rectify. It was time the mer-people forged a relationship with the land dwellers.

A gust of rain-scented wind blew through the dubious sanctuary and Wyn rolled onto his side. The breeze sent the clothes on the line to dancing. A few feet away, Nova lay on her right side, sound asleep with her hands tucked under her cheek. In repose, the fierce cat had been replaced with an exhausted kitten. Dark shadows marred the skin beneath her eyes and her long midnight hair confined in a braid accentuated her pale skin. Her features were delicate, which contradicted her prickly disposition. With her dark lashes and expressive blue eyes, Nova was easily the most beautiful woman he'd ever seen.

He smiled when he thought about mistaking her for a man. Who knew a woman would smoke a pipe? There was no way she could be mistaken for a man now.

Despite the blankets she was curled in, she shivered. The temperature had dropped in the past hour and the wind had picked up. The smart thing to do would be to stretch out beside her so they could share body warmth. But he hadn't seen her knife in a while and wasn't sure if she'd kept it near, though he'd hazard a guess she would. Warmth or not, he didn't want to wake with it buried in his chest.

In her slumber, she made a low noise and her hand clenched. Even in sleep, something tormented her.

Wyn rose, ignoring the protests from his abused body as he forced bruised muscles to respond. Spreading his blankets wide, he created a pallet for them both before adding more wood to the fire. He waited until the flames leapt high and hot before he approached her. Crouching, he scooped her up, blankets and all. Cradled in his arms, he carried her the few feet to his pallet.

He stopped just short of burying his nose in her fragrant hair as he placed her on the pallet. He'd never spent this much time with a human woman before and found he quite liked the experience. Her skin smelled of rain and reminded him of home.

He slid close behind her, then pulled the blankets over them both. With his chest to her back, he slid one arm around her slim waist. After a few moments, her shivers slowed and she leaned into him, still sound asleep. She murmured something and her hips wiggled against his groin, causing a rush of arousal to streak through his system.

He closed his eyes and allowed her scent to surround him. Mermen were highly sexed and it wasn't long until memories of making love crowded his mind. He tried to push away the lusty thoughts, but the vision of him entering her, taking her as a man takes a woman, were too powerful. His cock lengthened and thickened as shivers ran down his back and thighs. Just knowing she was nude beneath her blanket set his body on full alert.

He'd been in captivity a long time and, consequently, had allowed himself no release. Mermen were conditioned to have sex at least once a day, if not more, and his captors had wanted him to have sex while humans paid to watch him perform. He'd refused and been sorely beaten. In his world, sex was private, an act of mutual pleasure and procreation. It wasn't to be used for money or degradation.

Now that he was warm, well-fed and he held a beautiful, though mortal, woman in his arms, he could barely stand to lie motionless beside her. Inhaling the scent of her soft skin, he could only imagine the delicious anticipation of sinking into this woman's heat. Having her move beneath him, her strong thighs gripping his waist—

Swallowing a moan, he rolled out from under the blankets and rose to his feet. Stripping the blanket from his waist, he stalked into the driving rain, away from the woman who tempted him so. Walking the length of the ruins, he found a small sheltered area in the far corner. He climbed onto the wide ledge and pulled up his legs to brace his heels on the edge. With his back against the wall and his cock undaunted by the cold rain, he slid his hands around his thick shaft. His palm was already wet—it slid easily against his aroused flesh.

Through the overgrown weeds and vegetation, he could see Nova illuminated in the flickering firelight. He could imagine her full breasts—the sight of her in that corset had almost brought him to his knees. Would her nipples be big and round or small and tight? Would the thatch of her hair between her thighs be as dark as the hair on her head?

His eyes closed as powerful images washed over him. In desperation to remain silent, he bit his lip so hard he drew blood as he imagined sliding his cock into her body, her hands moving over him, stroking and caressing his flesh as she urged him on. Her thighs tight around him, her body damp and snug beneath him as he thrust again, again, again...

He clenched his eyes as the familiar sensation of orgasm overtook him. His testicles tightened as release gushed forth. He moaned against bloodied lips as wave after wave of release washed over him. Finally, as his tremors slowed, Wyn tipped his head back against the wall. His skin was cool and slick from the rain, but inside he was raging hot. He opened his eyes. While his body had found release, he still hungered for her.

CR SO

Nova came awake and, for once, it was a lovely feeling. Toasty warm in her blankets, she found it difficult to open her eyes for a change. Her body was still tired from the arduous journey of the day before but her mind was at peace. She stretched and thought about sleeping the day away—

Then a gentle male snore broke the serenity.

Her eyes flew open and her body tensed, ready to spring at the first sign of danger. Something warm slid across her belly and she shoved down the blankets to see a large male hand cupping her bare breast. Sometime during the night, her blanket sarong had abandoned her, leaving her nude in Wyn's arms. His big hand almost covered her entire breast and, between his thumb and forefinger, her nipple stood proudly erect. His fingers tightened and gave her a tender tweak that sent a shaft of heat down through her belly.

Wyn snored again and she scowled. The bastard was groping her in his sleep!

Her thighs tightened and she became aware of something poking her buttocks. She gave an experimental wiggle and felt his hips move against her in instant response. He mumbled something under his breath as he tweaked her nipple again. An answering heat spread through her abdomen and she automatically pushed against his groin with her hips. All she had to do was part her thighs and move back just a bit and he'd be in the perfect position to—

Dear Ola, what was she thinking?

Shocked at the lusty turn of her thoughts, she shoved his hand off her breast and rolled away. To her dismay, Wyn only scooted into her spot with a snore. He rubbed his face against the blanket before he settled and slept on undisturbed.

Bastard.

Nova rose, clad only in her drawers as her blanket was now trapped under her uninvited bed partner. Her body was stiff and she had numerous aches from the journey and a night spent on the ground. Grouchy because of her disturbed rest, she yanked her clothing from the line, pleased to see it was only slightly damp. After picking up her pack and boots, she slipped off for a few quiet moments to clean up and compose herself. If she remembered correctly, there was a small stream to the south where she'd be able to bathe.

She stomped through the thick rain-slick vegetation, her brow furrowed. How in the devil had she ended up in his bed anyway? The last thing she remembered was bedding down on the other side of the fire, which was definitely not where she'd found herself this morning. She rubbed her hand over her face. Why had he moved her? Did he think to seduce her?

She yanked her knife from her boot to slash at a thick vine that hampered her progress. She didn't want a man, not now, not ever. She'd spent the last year as a free woman and not once in that time had she wanted to take a man between her thighs. It wasn't because she thought all men were brutes. That wasn't the case. While a slave, she'd been lucky enough to have a master who'd taught her the pleasure her body was capable of. She just didn't want any man to have domination over her and, in her world, taking a lover would enable a man to do just that.

She shook her head. No, from now on Wyn would sleep on his own side of the fire and nowhere near hers.

Nova located the small stream and, since the water was cold, wasted no time in getting to work. As she scrubbed clean with her bathing cloth and soap, images of Wyn using the same items on his body flashed through her mind. Water running down his muscular frame, his skin sleek in the firelight—

The raucous cry of a crow startled her from her daydreams. Annoyed with her wandering lustful mind, she completed her bathing in record time. Thanks to fresh undergarments she located in the bottom of her bag, she could almost overlook the dampness of her outer clothing. She couldn't wait until they reached a town and she could rid herself of these clothes and purchase new ones. Fully dressed and feeling much more in control, she slung the pack over her shoulder. She'd wake him up, break their fast and be on their way. Within a day or so, she'd be home.

She headed up the hill at a brisk pace, eager to get moving, but when the abbey walls came into view she heard a wild whinny from the horse. She skidded to a stop and her hand automatically reached for her bodice knife. A shout sounded from the interior of the ruins and her heart leapt into her throat. Ignoring the lack of a path, she ran the rest of the way. The rain-soaked ground was treacherous underfoot and she almost lost her balance several times. When she reached the wall, she eased into position near a broken window to see into the ruins.

Nude, Wyn stood near their pallet, brandishing a large stick toward Evi's henchmen. Ber held a sword while Dreg carried a large fishing net. Her eyes narrowed when she saw the blood running down Wyn's arm.

Did these fools think to attack an unarmed man?

She slid the pack from her shoulder and dropped it beneath the window. Opening the front pocket, she removed a bola, a weapon made of a leather thong with two iron balls, one at each end. When thrown correctly, it could bring a grown man to his knees with the flick of a wrist.

"Come here, fish-man," Ber taunted. "I have something for you." The early morning light glinted off his sword.

As Nova slipped through the broken window, she unfurled the weapon. With deliberate steps, she moved forward. Dreg stepped toward Wyn and she swung the bola over her head several times, then released it. The weapon shot from her hand and flew through the air to catch Ber around the knees. The momentum of the iron balls twined the thong around his knees, trapping him.

"What the—!" Ber fell back with a crash and the sword flew from his grasp.

Wyn wasted no time and leapt on Dreg, using the element of surprise to take him down and tear the net from his grip. Nova ran forward and kicked Ber's sword out of reach. She slid her foot under the blade near the handle and flipped it high enough to catch it. She brought the blade around and aimed at his throat.

"Did Evi send you?"

"Fuck you," he snarled.

"Not on your life."

"Bitch," he snarled.

"So original." She pressed the tip of the sword against his chest and sliced through his shirt and the first few layers of skin. Blood welled to stain the material.

"I think we know why they're here," Wyn spoke. He grabbed Dreg on the nape of his neck and squeezed. After a few seconds, he sagged to the ground, unconscious. "I'll take care of him." He nodded toward Ber. "You go deal with their horses."

Nova backed away, taking care to remain out of Ber's reach. His legs were restrained but his arms were still free. "You might want to consider borrowing some of their clothing while you're at it," she said to Wyn.

"Good idea."

She ducked through the doorway and ran to the cart, the sword still in her hand. She found their attackers' horses tethered to a small bush around the corner of the abbey. Both animals were in fine shape and, other than identifying marks on the saddles, neither had been branded. Lucky for her because their lack of marks meant she could claim them as her own. These two would fetch a good sum.

She stripped the saddles and left them on the ground before she led the horses to the cart and secured their reins to the side rail. Taking them also made good sense. They would enable her to travel faster as they could switch the animals when one grew tired of pulling the cart.

She returned to the abbey and saw Wyn had secured both of the men with a section of clothesline. She was relieved to see he'd taken her advice and had relieved Ber of his clothing. He was dressed in dark trousers, knee boots and a white shirt stained with a small area of blood where she'd poked Ber in the chest. In his big hands, he held her bola.

"Sorry I ruined that shirt. It didn't occur to me until after I'd put a hole in it that you'd be able to use it," she said.

"It's nothing." He looked up. "Will you show me how to throw this weapon?"

"Only if you show me how you knocked him out." She nodded toward Dreg. "And after we put some distance between us and them." Ber was still conscious, though now stripped down to stained baggy drawers. He glared at her and she barely resisted the urge to stick out her tongue. She grabbed an armload of blankets. "How's your arm?"

"Just a scratch. We can deal with it later."

"As you wish."

She hurried past their prisoners to dump the blankets in the cart. There was no time to break their fast now, so they'd have to eat on the road. In a few short trips, she'd packed the wagon and retrieved her pack from under the window. When she returned to stow it in the cart, she found Wyn had already harnessed the mare to the cart.

"Are we ready?" She secured her pack under the seat.

"Almost. Shall I get rid of the sword?" He pointed to the weapon lying on the damp hay in the cart.

"No, we can sell it at the market in Wryven."

He nodded at the horses secured to the rails. "What about them? We aren't taking them, are we?"

"We sure are." Nova patted one on the rump. "They'll fetch a good price."

He cocked his head. "Is that all you think about...money?"

She climbed into the driver's seat. "No. I think about food, too."

Chapter Five

Wyn stood on the cliff, his hands on his hips as he gazed across the inlet and miles of open sea below. To the south was his island home, CasadUne in the land of Rom de Mer. The scent of salty water was making him delirious and it took all of his restraint to keep from jumping off the cliffs and into the water. While he couldn't wait to feel the embrace of his beloved ocean again, first he had to deal with Nova's house. Or what was left of it.

For the past day and a half, they'd pushed themselves and the horses to their limits. They'd taken turns driving while the other huddled in the back of the cart to snatch much-needed sleep. They'd made few stops and the last had been in the village market of Wryven, about an hour to the north. After selling the sword, their attackers' horses and her clothes, Nova had purchased fresh food, clothes for both of them and several bags of feed for the mare. Other than a lack of shelter, they should be set for a few days.

Wyn walked to the front of the house and eyed the structure critically. Surely she didn't mean to live *here*. This place was unfit for animals, let alone humans. Other than the fact that this hovel commanded an impressive view of the ocean, he could see no other redeeming factor. For the most part, the walls looked sound, though there were significant cracks that needed immediate attention. Crafted of peach-colored stone, the sinking sun set the walls ablaze with its fading rays. The roof had long since caved in and the resulting mess would have to be cleared before anything else could be done. In reality, this venture was well beyond his abilities and, even with experienced help, the work would take weeks before someone could live here.

He turned to tell Nova what he thought of her home when her expression stopped him dead. She was staring at the wreckage with such longing that it was almost painful to watch. Her eyes were damp with tears and her lower lip trembled. She stood with her arms wrapped around her waist as if to comfort herself.

He crossed his arms over his chest, then looked at the house again. Okay, it had possibilities, but it would take a lot of work to make it habitable. If this was what she wanted, he'd do everything in his power to make it so. It was the least he could do for her.

"We need to set up camp," he said. "I'll gather wood if you can clear a place to build the fire."

She gave him an absent nod, her gaze still fixed on the house. He had no idea what she saw, but whatever it was, it had captured her attention. Leaving her alone with her thoughts, Wyn found an overgrown path leading from the cliff to the beach. With every step, his heart rate increased with the anticipation of submerging himself in the sea. Soon he was running down the path, shedding his clothes as he went. In no time at all, he was nude and sprinting for the water.

With a wild shout, he dove into the waves and warm water closed over his head. The salt stung his wounds, but he ignored the pain. Nothing could compare to the sheer ecstasy of the water's embrace. For a few moments, he simply floated, allowing the reality of being in the sea to merge with the dreams he'd had while in captivity. His dreams hadn't come close.

He let out a joyous whoop and allowed his body to sink beneath the waves. Stretching, he began to swim. The going was slow at first as his abused body resisted the natural movements, but soon the pain faded and, aided by the webbing of his hands and feet, he raced around the inlet with ease. He swam in dizzying circles, then along the beach and around the point of Maragorn, more than a mile from Nova's home.

When his heart was content, he returned to shore, his body tired from traveling and the swim. A year ago, he could have swum for miles without tiring. Being forced to remain on land had taken away his edge but now he was almost home. If he looked to the south, he could imagine the spires of his island.

He strode from the water onto the beach, shaking off droplets as he moved. He'd help Nova put her house in order and then he'd be free to go and all would be as it should.

He ignored the queer little jerk in his gut at the thought of leaving her. She was an amazing woman—intelligent, tough and a bit prickly. He grinned as he pulled on his trousers. And he couldn't wait to get back to her.

On his way up the path, he collected an armload of driftwood. This would be more than enough to keep them warm for the night. Once they started working on the house, they'd be able to burn small pieces of the roof for their fire.

The sun had almost set by the time he returned and Nova had constructed a stone fire ring on the west side, giving them a broad view of the ocean and sunset.

She sat in the back of the cart, pawing through the basket of provisions as she whistled an off-key tune. She'd changed into a white blouse and leaf-green skirt that left her feet and calves bare as she swung them in an energetic fashion. With her hair unbound, she looked as if she hadn't a care in the world. So unlike a few hours ago. Beside her sat an open bottle of wine.

"I thought you'd never come back." She pulled an apple out of the basket. "It looked like you were going to swim back home."

Wyn dropped the wood near the fire ring. He'd thought about leaving her and swimming home, but knew he couldn't go back on his word. He owed her. "I said I'd help you get your house in order."

"And I appreciate that." She took a noisy bite of the fruit. "You can really swim fast. Probably faster than anyone I've ever seen."

He dropped into a crouch and constructed a stubby pyramid of twigs before tucking dried grass around the base. He froze when the fading sunlight reflected on the gossamer webbing between his fingers. He clenched his hand into a fist. "Nova, I have something to tell you." He raised his head and their gazes met. "I'm not human."

"No foolin'?" She cocked her head, her expression curious. "Well, you look human to me. I once saw a man change into a cougar. Can you do that?"

He couldn't help but grin. He shouldn't have been surprised that she hadn't batted a lash at his statement. Judging from the fact she was a gambler, she'd probably seen many things a gently reared woman would never have been privy to. Though, for someone as tough as she was, she possessed a sense of innocence about her that couldn't be ignored.

"No, I'm a merman."

"What's a merman?" She took another bite of the apple while her legs continued an energetic rhythm.

"My people come from the sea."

"So you're like a fish?"

"Yes."

Her gaze dropped to his legs, then back to his face. "You're fooling me—"

"Well, I didn't mean literally." He added a few more sticks to the pile. "My clan doesn't live in the sea though some still do. We have an island south of here."

"Can you show me?" Nova hopped off the back of the cart with her ever-present pack in hand. She paused to grab the wine bottle. "I want to see you in the water up close."

"Maybe in the morning, not now."

She dropped to a crouch across the fire ring from him, her skirt settling on the ground in a swirl of color. "I've never heard of any such thing." She rooted in her bag until she pulled out a small flint. "And I won't believe it until I see it." She tossed it at him.

"Have you ever seen a liter of deuces?" he asked.

She shook her head.

"You haven't seen it, but do you doubt it exists?"

The surprise on her face was almost comical and he grinned. She wanted to object, he could see it in her eyes, but she had no reply because he was correct. Just because one hadn't seen it, didn't mean something didn't exist.

"Is that why they're after you, because you're a merman?"

"Yes." He held the flint near the base of his pyramid, then struck the flint several times before leaning forward to blow softly on the little sparks that danced in the dried grasses.

"How did you become a slave?"

He indicated she should wait while he concentrated on the tiny embers. Within a few minutes, the grasses had caught and the flames raced toward the twigs. He sat back.

"My clan lives on an island called CasadUne not far from here and we don't associate with the land dwellers very often. But there are times when we come ashore to barter or enjoy a taste of your civilization." He looked to the final rays of the sun streaking the sky with dark pinks and purples. "There's nothing more compelling than a sunset, is there?"

She took a drink of wine then offered him the bottle. "And you were caught while watching a sunset?"

"Not quite." He took the offering and raised the bottle to his lips. He'd never had human wine before. The fruity, slightly sweet taste spread through his mouth as he swallowed the dark liquid. "I'd been traveling for hours and was tired. I'd come ashore to bask in the warmth of the nooning sun. I had climbed onto the rocks and fallen asleep and I woke with a net over me." He took another drink. "I was hauled to the slave market and bought." He lowered the bottle as he considered the unexpected effects of the drink. After a few moments, he decided the warmth spreading through his system was quite...enjoyable.

"By Evi?"

"Yes."

"What did he want with you?"

"To make money." The anger he felt at being paraded before the slave buyers raced to the fore and he could feel his skin flush. How anyone could treat another being with such a lack of compassion was beyond him. "He charged people to see me swim, then charged extra to touch me."

"And that's why he beat you, isn't it?" She took a drink from the bottle and handed it back. "Because you fought him?"

Wyn nodded. "I'm not some quirk of nature to be towed from town to town locked in a wagon. He didn't see me as a person with feelings and emotions and neither did the people who paid to touch me. Money means nothing if someone gets hurt in the process." He spat.

Nova turned her face toward the sunset, her expression distant.

"He was making plans to sell me to a land dweller woman who wanted to use me as her jaJin, her pleasure bearer. I wouldn't be free to come and go, I'd be her sexual slave." He raised the bottle to his lips, enjoying the warmth the liquid delivered to his gut. The more he drank, the farther he could distance himself from the pain and humiliation of his imprisonment.

She shook her head. "Why would he do that? I mean, in any of the larger cities anyone can hire a jaJin and it's socially acceptable behavior—"

"Mermen are known for being exceptionally...sensual."

Her eyes widened and her gaze dropped to his crotch, then up again. "In what way?"

"For instance, we can maintain an erection for hours at a time thus guaranteeing a woman multiple orgasms."

Nova snorted and shook her head. "The ability to hammer away for hours does not guarantee an orgasm."

"It is if the man knows how to do it right," he boasted.

She rolled her eyes. "All men think they do it 'right'. Luckily for us women, we know better."

"You're jaded."

"No, just realistic." She rose to retrieve another bottle of wine from the basket in the cart. "Most men think with their cocks. Unfortunately, it usually gives bad information."

"Says who?"

"Says me."

She resumed her seat and removed the cork with the tip of her dagger. When she took a deep drink of the ruby liquid, a drop ran down her chin and Wyn was seized with the desire to lick it off.

"Besides, if men knew how to do it properly, there would be no prostitution," she said.

"Why do you say that?" He tossed the old bottle behind him as he enjoyed the floaty sensation in his head. Maybe he needed to eat something.

"If they knew how to use their equipment properly, then most women wouldn't be adverse to sex." Nova leaned over to rummage in the food basket.

He shook his head. "Most women aren't—"

"Many women are." She tossed him a chunk of white cheese.

"Yourself included?" He caught the food as well as the flash of indecision on her face. Something bad had happened in her past and it held her back even now.

"We weren't talking about me. Besides, I'm different." She shrugged. "I choose not to have sex."

"And why is that?" He bit into the cheese, enjoying the sharp, flavorful bite. Never had he tasted such wonderful cheese...

"Sex is about power—"

"What?" He almost bit his tongue.

She nodded and he could see her movements weren't quite as precise as they'd been before. The wine was having as much of an effect on her as it was on him.

"I don't know how it is in your world, but in the human world sex is about power. Men use the power of sexual attraction to control their mates while women use it to get what they want." She pulled a loaf of bread out of the basket and tore it in half. "If women withhold sex from their mate, invariably the men come running back at some point." She tossed half of the bread at him. "Or they go out and buy it."

He caught the bread and set it on one of the rocks near the fire to warm. "Your view of sex is twisted. If you look at your society, speaking sexually of course, the jaJin are the ones who have it made. By their own consent, they willingly engage in sex and they receive cash for their work as well as the pleasure in giving satisfaction to another."

She snorted. "Men do not receive satisfaction in giving pleasure."

"I do."

"Uh huh." Her tone was disbelieving.

He leaned toward her. "It's true. I receive almost as much satisfaction from giving pleasure as receiving it. Obviously I receive physical pleasure from an orgasm, but I receive divine gratification from bringing release to a woman."

She cocked her head and her pupils were large, making her eyes appear darker, more vulnerable. "Are all mermen like you?"

"Most."

"Well," she laughed, "I shall seek your kind when I decide to take a lover."

A slow burn began in his gut at the thought of this woman taking a lover. The thought of another man kissing her full lips, caressing her breasts and the soft hair between her beautiful thighs. Another man entering her, taking her, bringing her to satisfaction.

Another man loving her.

"What's wrong with right now?" he asked.

She put down the bottle and tore off a bite of bread. "Right now, what?"

"Let's make love."

"Now?" She gulped.

The expression in her dark eyes spoke volumes. Fear and curiosity warred in their blue depths. Her breathing accelerated and through her thin blouse he could see her erect nipples. She was aroused, and even though they were separated by a foot or so, he could smell her heat. He ached to touch her, taste her essence.

"Meet me halfway, Nova. Let me prove what I can do for you."

Her dark lashes fluttered and she swallowed, hard.

"If you're shy, I can come to you—"

"Who said I was shy?" A mutinous look crossed her face.

He fought the urge to grin. This woman was proud, very proud. "If you're scared—"

"You think I'm scared?" She lunged at him for a brief punishing kiss. But, before he could get a good taste of her, she backed away. "I'll take a lover when I decide the time is right. You can't goad me into it." She grabbed the front of his shirt and pulled him onto his knees. Up close, he was assailed by her fragrance. Her eyes were dilated and she licked her lips, drawing his attention to her mouth. "Maybe you should be afraid of me, merman." Her voice dropped. "I *am* a very accomplished lover."

He cupped her hips and brought her closer. Her eyes widened as he pressed his burgeoning erection into her stomach. They were a perfect fit.

He slid his hand beneath her skirt, his palm hot against her thigh. "I am not afraid of any woman." His words were brave, but he wasn't at all sure that this woman didn't scare him to death.

He dipped his head and his lips brushed hers—once, twice. It was more of a tease than an actual kiss and he wanted inside her mouth, he needed a taste of her. His tongue snaked out and just as it touched her lips, she shoved him backward. He went down on his back, and with a soft cry, she flung herself on top of him. He grasped her by the hips and rolled her beneath him, their legs tangled as they moved. If he didn't taste her soon, he'd explode. He swooped and captured her mouth. Hot and sweet, she opened and took him deep, her tongue wrestling with his as her busy hands worked to remove his shirt.

Their kiss was wet and greedy as they ate at each other's mouths. A soft moan sounded from her throat and she sucked his tongue, driving sensation directly to his throbbing groin. She nipped his lower lip before breaking the kiss to tear at the buttons on his pants.

He braced his hands on the ground and pushed to give her better access. With her eyes wild and her lips swollen from his kisses, she was magnificent and he wanted to tell her so.

"You're beautiful."

To his surprise, she scowled at him. "You don't have to seduce me with pretty words, Wyn."

She released her grip on his pants to tangle her fingers in his hair and drag his mouth back to hers. Together, they rolled across the ground until he ended up on the bottom—each struggling to touch and taste more of the other. He felt as if he couldn't get enough of her. Like a starving man, he wanted to spread her across the ground and feast on her. Her nipples would taste of—

J.C. Wilder

All thoughts of seduction flew from his mind as her hand plunged into the front of his pants and her fingers encircled his cock. She squeezed gently, causing sparks to arc before his eyes. She certainly had talented hands, and if she didn't stop, he wouldn't last long enough to enjoy any other part of her. And he wanted to so very badly.

Panting, he reached for her wrists. "You have too many clothes on."

A wicked smile curved her kiss-swollen lips. "I can take care of that."

She sat up, her thighs parted to bracket his hips. Grasping her shirt, she pulled it over her head and tossed it aside. Her full breasts bounded free and he reached for her. Shaking her head, she gave him a saucy smile that further heated his blood. She rose to her feet and removed her skirt.

She was magnificent.

His cock gave a twitch as if in invitation and she slipped to her knees over him, this time wrapping her hand around the base of his cock. Adjusting herself, she positioned him at her entrance and, with a heady sigh, sank him deep.

He captured her hips and adjusted her angle, catching her clitoris dead on. A moan broke from her lips as she drew her thighs tight to his hips, rubbing her lower body against him. Each tiny movement wrought an answering noise from her throat. She caught his hands and placed them on her breasts, showing him exactly how she liked to be touched.

Then she began to move.

Head tipped back, she lifted her body from his only to return, barely giving him time to draw breath. With a dreamy smile on her face, she moved easily, her body rocking in harmony with his as her pace increased. The tips of her silken hair tickled his legs when suddenly she tightened around him, straining, coming apart over him.

He gritted his teeth as her orgasm caressed his cock. It was too fast. He wanted to savor her, touch every inch of her skin. He wanted it to last for hours, not minutes.

But Nova wasn't done yet.

She gave a hum of satisfaction when her soft, questing fingers caressed his nipples. With lips swollen and damp, eyes luminous with her release, a wicked smile blossomed as she swooped to capture a hardened nub between her teeth. Rocking her hips, she suckled him with abandon and he was lost.

With a cry, he grabbed her hips and hammered into her. Sensation raged through his body as she teased him with her mouth. Sounds of delight escaped her throat as she met him thrust for thrust, her body surrounding him in wet heat.

She released him and sat up, taking his cock deeper and that was all it took. Hands tight on her hips, he held her in place as he came hard. Within seconds, she tensed over him, her voice mingling with his as she convulsed around him once more.

Nova collapsed over him, her thick dark hair blanketing them. He stroked her back, and a few moments later, he realized she'd fallen asleep. He stared up at the dark sky and noticed something was poking him in the back, but he was too stunned to move.

What in the world had just happened between them?

Chapter Six

The cool sea breeze did little to lower the temperature of Nova's overheated skin. The sun was high overhead and they'd been working hard to remove debris from the interior of the house since sunup. Even though the work was grueling, nothing could prevent the thrill of homecoming that raced through her every time she stepped across the threshold.

Thunk!

Out of the corner of her eye, she saw Wyn in the far corner near the collapsed fireplace. He was chopping the massive beams that had once supported the roof. He'd removed his shirt and his muscular body was drenched in sweat. As he brought down the ax, the play of muscles and sinew was mesmerizing. Her tongue grew thick. Her breasts tingled and her skin grew moist. Since their encounter last evening, every breath seemed deeper and fuller, making her more aware of her body than ever before.

Would she lie with him again?

Yes...

Her cheeks flushed and she stooped to gather another load of wood, then hurried outside, her arms full of manageable pieces of what had once been her roof.

Ever since last night's earth-shattering events, she hadn't been able to look him in the eye. Luckily she didn't have to speak as he'd already been hard at work when she'd awoken. Other than a hurried nod, they hadn't communicated at all unless it was to shout a warning or give instruction.

She strode to the pile of refuse at the side of the house. Never had she responded to a man as she had last night. Never had it been so...hot. Then again, rarely had a man taken the time to arouse her before. Most men didn't care if their slaves felt anything during sex; they were only interested in achieving their own satisfaction.

She dropped the armload of wood and her breath caught as a splinter tore through her gloves. Disgusted, she tore off the glove to inspect the damage. Blood oozed from the wound and a good-sized splinter stuck out of the palm of her hand. She swore beneath her breath and picked at it with her ragged fingernails.

"What did you do?"

Hearing his voice so close startled her and she drove the wood deeper into her palm. She swore again.

"Are you hurt?"

Before she could answer, he took her hand in his. Warmth radiated along her hand and up her arm, and her breasts ached.

"A splinter. Nasty business when doing work like this." Without releasing her hand, he led her to their camp.

"I can take care of it." She tried to pull away but he didn't release her.

"It's easier if I do it. These can be tricky one-handed." He pushed her down on a makeshift bench he'd made from a roof support earlier in the day. "You don't want it to get infected."

He gathered a bottle of fresh water and a rag and began cleaning her hand. As he worked, her gaze caught on the clean, light strands of his hair. His hair was bound at the back of his neck with a strip of leather. The two braids were still in place and they swung with his movements, accompanied by a soft click as the shells struck each other.

His touch was gentle and he smelled of male sweat, seawater and sunshine. Already his wounds were healing and his frame was filling out. Her gaze moved over the rippling muscles of his arms and shoulders. Arousal beat slow and steady beneath her skin.

"Your wounds are healing well." Her voice came out husky and she felt breathless.

His blond head came up and his gaze met hers. "Yes," he said. "Now that I'm back near the ocean, I'll heal soon enough." He returned his attention to her hand. Once the wound was clean, he asked for her knife.

"What do you need it for?" She pulled the weapon from her boot and handed it to him.

"I need to make a small cut to get the splinter out. You've pushed it in too far."

"I've already said I can take care of—"

"Don't worry." His gaze was teasing. "I'll not cut off your hand. I've had plenty of practice in removing splinters." He cleaned the blade with fresh water and a clean cloth.

She frowned. "Does one get a lot of splinters as a merman?"

"Not like humans." He made a tiny incision and her breath caught. "But we have wickedly sharp coral and sometimes the spines will embed themselves and have to be dug out."

He dipped his head and she jerked as his lips touched her palm. He sucked at the wound and her toes curled at the sensuality of the action. His lips and tongue were soft, and after several pulls, he raised his head. His mouth was stained with her blood and between his gritted teeth was the splinter. He spat it into the fire ring.

"Thank you."

He poured water into his hand, then rinsed his mouth. "It is I who should be thanking you."

"For what?"

"Saving me." He poured a liberal amount of water over her palm. "For giving me my life back."

"Well, you already thanked me and you don't have your life back—"

"Yet, but I will." He dried her hand with one of the cloths and applied some of the wound salve. "Evi kept a tight rein and I didn't know how I could get away, though I knew at some point I'd have to. To remain in captivity was not an option." He grinned. "Little did I know I'd achieve freedom with the help of an ebony-headed enchantress."

Nova laughed. "I think you were hit on the head one too many times." Never had she been called an enchantress by any stretch of the imagination.

"And I think you underestimate yourself." He gave her hand a pointed look. "You'll need to take it easy for the rest of the day."

"We still have a lot of work to do—"

"But not now. It's well past nooning and we've had nothing substantial to eat. I think we should grab something and head down to the beach. A quick swim and sustenance will set us to rights." He loomed over her and offered his hand.

Nova stared at it, his broad palm, the numerous lines crisscrossing it. It was a strong hand. A capable hand. He turned it ever so slightly and the light caught on the iridescent webbing between his fingers. Reverently, she touched the skin between his thumb and forefinger. It was thin and pliable and, when he stretched his fingers apart to allow her a better inspection, the skin sparkled like the surface of an opal. It was beautiful yet alien at the same time. It was also another reason she couldn't lose her heart. They were as different as night and day.

She slid her hand into his and allowed him to help her to her feet. Together they gathered supplies for lunch and packed everything into a basket. Wyn carried it while she followed with one of the blankets. They walked down the path and onto the narrow slice of beach. The sand was warm beneath her feet and he led her to a sheltered area beneath a large tree at the very base of the cliffs.

"I say we swim first." He tucked the basket into a shaded corner near a rock.

She looked out to sea. The sunlight cast thousands of sparkles across the gentle waves. This place held hundreds of memories for her...and they were almost all good ones for a change.

"I say you're on," she said.

Feeling like a child set free, she stripped to a thin chemise and long-legged drawers then ran to the water. Behind her she could hear Wyn close behind. When he drew near, he made a playful grab for her arm and she shied away with a shriek. Racing for the sea, she dove without a backward glance.

The water was warm and embraced her like a second skin. Taking a deep breath, she plunged beneath the surface and into the blue-green depths. Here the world was silent and peaceful— there was no one to bother her, just fish and water.

She rose to the surface only when her lungs felt near to bursting. She'd take in huge gulps of fresh air then return to the watery depths to swim among the fish and rock formations.

She marveled at what it must mean to live as Wyn and his people lived. It would be a beautiful uncomplicated world with a slow pace.

She broke the surface near a large multi-leveled boulder in the center of the lagoon. She shook water from her eyes and saw Wyn on top of the rock as nude as the day he was born. His body glinted with water droplets and his sex hung heavy between his spread thighs. He looked relaxed and sexy, and a slow warmth blossomed in her belly. She wanted to lie with him again. The gentle nature he'd shown in the past two days had proved to her that he was a man who could be trusted with her body, if not her heart.

"You swim well for a land dweller," he said.

"My mother and grandmother taught me." She swam closer. "In this very place."

"Really?"

She nodded. "That wreck of a house is where my mother was born, and her mother before her."

"And that's why you want to live here."

She nodded, her gaze fixed on the house above. "It's the only place I've ever called home. Some of the best memories of my life are of swimming and fishing right here."

"What happened?"

She pulled her gaze away, reluctant to talk about what had happened so many years ago. "It doesn't matter now." She found a foothold and climbed the side of the rock until she stood at his feet. As she touched his knee, he straightened, his gaze sharp, aware.

"You keep telling me that I'm beautiful," she said. "But you're beautiful as well."

He gave her a lazy smile as his fingers encircled her wrist. "Do you think so?'

"Yes."

"Well now, it's a beautiful sunny day. We're here alone on our small island." He indicated the rock they sat on. "What do you think two beautiful people should do together?"

"Mmm." She allowed herself to be pulled into his lap. Against her hip, his cock grew hard. "Make bread? Play Goddess and Dragons? Maybe—" Her words ended in a hiss as he nipped her earlobe.

"Hush, woman."

His mouth covered hers and she dissolved into a warm puddle as their tongues sought each other. Her arms slid around his neck and they suckled each other's mouths. Giving herself to the sensuality he offered, she stroked the warm skin of his upper back and neck. His wet hair covered her hands like warm silk and she tangled her fingers in it.

His hands stroked a lazy path up her back and she moaned as he cupped her breast. His thumb teased her nipple into erect awareness. He broke the kiss and mumbled against her jaw, "I think you're wearing too many clothes again."

Nova's sigh turned to a gasp as he swung her off his lap and onto the rock beside him. He removed her chemise and tossed it into the ocean.

"You know, I don't have very many clothes," she complained.

"Who needs clothes?" he asked.

"I do, for one." She laughed as he nuzzled her neck and hit a particularly sensitive spot. He urged her hips upward and slid her drawers down her legs and tossed them in the sea as well.

She gave them a mournful glance. "I think you're hard on my wardrobe."

He sat cross-legged and pulled her into his lap to straddle him. His cock was pressed against the damp apex of her thighs. "No, I think I'm hard for you."

Her laughter turned to a sigh as he moved his hips against her and his cock rubbed against her woman's mound. They kissed again, their bodies as close together as they could get without him actually entering her. Their hands stroked and caressed every inch of flesh they could reach. He cupped her breast and his thumb teased the taut peak with a slow touch.

"You have beautiful breasts."

Nova ran her palms over his flat nipples and teased them into sharp little points. She was pleased when his breath left him in a hiss as she scraped her nails over them.

He leaned back, his eyes smoky with need. "I want to taste them."

Her eyelids drooped as his tongue flicked over one nipple, then the other. Taking one into his mouth, he sucked hard and wrenched a cry from her. His wicked caresses continued and the dampness between her thighs increased with each teasing action. Beneath her, Wyn moved his hips in a restless manner and she wasn't sure he was even aware he was doing it.

Her fingers tangled in his hair, holding him hostage against her breast though he didn't seem to want to leave anytime soon. Her hips picked up his rhythm and increased the friction against her clitoris. She tipped back her head, need riding low and hard in her abdomen as she bore down on his cock while his tongue continued its magic.

Spasms of heat streaked up her thighs as her body clenched and she screamed his name as she gained release. His hands cupped her hips, steadying her as she lost control.

Dimly, she was aware of him speaking in low encouraging tones, but she couldn't focus on his words. Limp, her head sank to rest on his shoulder while pleasurable aftershocks still reverberated through her body.

Once the storm had passed, she roused and raised her head from his shoulder. Her body hummed with satisfaction and his cock still prodded her.

She gave him a sleepy smile. "You look like you could use some help here, my friend."

He looked pained. "Yes, please."

She slid her hand around his cock, luxuriating in the silk and steel of him. As she stroked, his eyes dilated and he gave himself into her seduction. Needing lubrication, she ran her hand between her thighs until her fingers were damp with cream. She smoothed her moisture over his cock, paying careful attention to his broad head. His eyes slid closed and his hips followed her every movement. He strained beneath her and his breathing grew short and heavy. He moaned and his hips jerked as he came, his come shooting up to coat her breasts and belly.

She released him to rub the essence of their experience into her skin. Into her breasts, her nipples and her stomach. She raised her head to see him watching her erotic play.

She smiled and plumped her breasts with both hands. "Care for a taste?"

CR SO

"What do you mean, you lost them?" Evi slammed his fist on the table. "This is unacceptable. Do you have any idea how much money that creature is worth?"

Ber and Dreg shook their heads. They really were a pathetic twosome. Dreg had a large knot on his head while Ber was dressed in something that resembled a window drape embroidered with pink flowers.

Fools.

"He's worth a small ransom to me and I'm paying you handsomely to find him. Now go and don't return until you have something better to report."

The men left the room and Evi sank into his chair. The Countess Pont le Neve was impatiently waiting in the wings to claim the merman. The money she was willing to pay would set Evi up for life. His fist clenched, then relaxed. He couldn't lose out now; he'd been poor far too long to give up.

He picked up a small bell and rang it. Almost immediately the door opened and a half-naked jaJin entered. Slim and blonde with a gold belt holding up a sheer skirt, she carried a tray of fruit and wine. Her gaze was bold and she gave him a wide smile.

"Are you ready to eat, milord?"

Chapter Seven

Nova was a thing of beauty to behold as she emerged from the sea. Her dark hair was slicked back and water droplets ran down her body. Her breasts and hips swayed with a sensuality he knew she was unaware of and his cock swelled in response. Their gazes met and a warm blush moved over her cheeks before she looked away.

After their interlude on the rock, they'd swum back to the beach and eaten their lunch. Consisting mainly of bread, cheese and wine, they'd taken turns feeding each other small morsels of food until replete. After they'd taken a short nap, Nova had opted for a quick dip to rinse off the sand.

"Shall we get back to work?" She reached for her blouse on the blanket next to him.

"You're a hard taskmaster." He gave a lazy yawn, well aware of the quick glances she'd been giving his cock. "And I have a better idea." He grabbed the hem of her shirt and tugged.

"I need to get dressed—"

She resisted his attempts to take her shirt and he resorted to grabbing her wrist before pulling her down next to him. "I don't know about you, but I'm far too full to go back to work immediately." He rolled with her until she was beneath him.

Her brow arched and a playful smile curved her mouth. "Indeed?" She slid her arms around his shoulders. "What did you have in mind?"

"Mmm, how about spending the rest of the afternoon here?" He slid his knee between her legs and she opened for him. "In only a few hours, it will be time to eat again..." He settled his hips between her thighs and his cock rested against her woman's mound. "And I have a few more things I'd like to do with you." He traced the curve of her brow with a fingertip. "For you." He followed the line of her cheek. "And to you." He tickled her lower lip with his nail. Her lips parted and he dipped his finger inside, surprised when she reciprocated by nipping his fingertip.

His eyes narrowed as heat rushed through his loins and he removed his finger. He lowered his head and nibbled her dampened lips. Sucking the lower one between his teeth, he released her after a tender nip. He kissed and sucked his way down her throat while she twisted as if to try and maneuver him in a particular direction.

But he had his own agenda.

Keeping his pace lazy, he seduced each shoulder, stroking and caressing her sun-warmed flesh. She would have to be careful to not get burned, her pale skin was already turning pink from exposure to the sun. He kissed his way between her breasts, enjoying the flavor of sea and woman.

Bracing himself on one arm, he stroked the generous curve of one breast. Already her nipples were semi-hard and begging for his touch. He licked his finger and drew a damp circle around her areola and her nipple tightened. Her breasts were so responsive, he wondered if he could bring her off by touching them alone. He licked his finger again and painted her nipple with his saliva. Her breathing deepened and he took the tight point into his mouth. He suckled deeply, wrenching a cry from her. Her hands tangled in his hair as he seduced her with his mouth.

Smiling at her breathy sounds, he kissed his way down her abdomen stopping only to nuzzle her belly button. Her flesh was warm and soft as silk, her thighs open as he moved down her body. The soft dark hair covering her woman's mound was damp with desire. He opened her to stroke wet flesh as he dipped his head to taste her.

Her hips thrust against him as his tongue sought her clitoris. She cried as his fingers penetrated. Her fists knotted in his hair and her hips arched against his mouth. She moaned and unrestrained desire had aroused him to the point of pain.

"I have to have you," he muttered. He rose above her, his cock full, its tip damp with pre-come. He dipped the head of his cock into her slick flesh, gritting his teeth when he felt how tight she was. Sweat broke across his brow as he pressed forward, his head disappearing into her sweet body.

"Wyn...please..."

She moaned when he thrust forward and buried himself in her body. His teeth came together hard as she flexed. Her hands moved to his hips and she urged him on. He withdrew, then entered again with a slow thrust. He braced his weight on his arms and his head fell back. The sense of rightness was unbelievable. As he sank deep again, the wet suck of her flesh around his cock aroused him more than ever. He increased his pace and began to thrust in deep, even strokes.

Together they rode the peak, her body tightening beneath his as she screamed out her satisfaction. His balls constricted, release just seconds away. He moaned and his hips jerked sporadically as wave after wave of sensation tore through his body.

Exhausted and gasping for air, he let his head drop beside hers.

Had sex ever been this powerful with another woman?

ରେ ৪০

A week later, the sun was setting as Nova guided her horse toward home. The dying light cast a pinkish golden glow over everything and, for once, the thought of home didn't bring the feeling of satisfaction as it once had. Thanks to the Wryven workers she'd hired, the walls were patched and the roof was almost complete. Within a few days, she'd be done.

And Wyn would leave...

As if her thoughts had conjured him, he emerged from the house with a wheelbarrow of scrap lumber. For once he had his shirt on but had left it open to expose his chest. He hauled the debris to a large fire and dumped it in. A wild shower of sparks rose high above the flames. He stood, bare-chested and powerful like a pagan god of old. Her toes curled.

He isn't yours to keep...

She frowned. Did she really want a man around all the time? Sooner or later he'd expect her to cook for him and wash his clothes, then let him fuck her whenever and wherever he decided. It wouldn't matter if she were ill or busy, he'd expect her to pull up her skirts and let him—

Wyn isn't like that...

True, he hadn't acted like any man she'd ever known. But he was still a man and they weren't to be trusted. She turned her attention to the path and urged the horse onward. Once everything was done, he'd be free to go and she could get on with her life as well.

"You'll never guess what I unearthed while you were gone," he called as she approached.

"What?" She slowed the horse.

"This." He waved toward a jumble of items near the front door.

She handed him a bundle of provisions before she slid off the horse. Lined up beside the threshold were a kitchen table, three chairs and a small lopsided table that her grandmother had used for sewing. She dropped to her knees and ran her hands reverently over the scarred tabletop. She remembered her granny sitting in her rocker beside the small table for many hours, creating the most amazing embroidery. Nova's hand shook as she opened the little drawer in front. She'd kept her floss here, neatly aligned by color and hue, and they'd dazzled a little girl who'd had very little color in her life until then. Except for a few cobwebs, the drawer was empty.

Much like her life.

She cleared her throat. "Where did you find this?"

"In the shed out back. These are the only salvageable pieces... They can be cleaned and used again."

"That they can be." She shut the drawer. "I'll add that to my list." She grinned at him then walked into the house. The main room was empty and the floors had been swept clean with the broom she'd purchased on her last trip to town. The fireplace had been cleared as well as the areas that had served as the kitchen and bedroom. Last night she'd stashed her wealth in a niche in the fireplace, the very same place her granny had kept her money. It was truly becoming her home.

It seemed strange to be standing here again. When her family had left so many years ago, her father had sworn that none of his blood would ever set foot here again.

How wrong he'd been.

She ran her hands over the pockmarked wood of the fireplace mantel. The pattern of sea waves and shells carved into the mantel was as familiar as her own face. The wood had taken a beating, but with time and effort, most of it could be salvaged. Her grandfather, a man she'd never known, had carved this for his new bride. She traced the curve of a shell. Here was the history of her family. Here was her past—the part she wanted to remember anyway.

"What is this place to you?"

Wyn's quiet question jolted her out of reverie and she turned her hand to inspect her dusty fingers. She rubbed them together.

"I told you, my mother and grandmother were born here." She offered him a smile and hoped he'd drop the subject.

He shook his head. "It's more than that. The expression on your face tells me you have more than just a familial connection to this place. It's something deeper, more intrinsic to who you are and where you've been."

He saw too much.

Uncomfortable, she turned toward the south window. Through the glassless openings, the sea beckoned and a fresh breeze blew. Her grandmother had had white cotton curtains and windows that opened inward. In warm weather, she'd always kept the windows open to catch the scent of the sea.

"My mother married beneath her." Her words were rusty and she was surprised at how much effort it took to form them. "You can see from this place that she grew up in relatively humble surroundings. My grandfather died when she was but a child.

"After his death, my grandmother earned money with her sewing and embroidery. She wanted to make sure that mama had everything she'd ever need and she sacrificed a great deal for her only child." She leaned against the windowsill. "I can still see her sitting here at this window as she sewed.

"My mother was young when she met my father. I don't know much about their relationship other than my grandmother did not support it." Her lip curled. "That fact sticks in my father's throat to this day."

"He's still alive?"

She snorted. "One would assume so. He's too rotten to die easily." She shrugged. "He and his brothers, sons of the magistrate from the province of Lethoria, were raised to know how to use their fists. Because they could be charming, they also learned at an early age how to scam.

"Anyway, my parents met, they married and soon she was pregnant with me. That's when everything began to sour. My father and his brothers were arrested for cheating at cards. While it isn't a crime per se, one of their marks was the son of an Overseer." She gave a humorless chuckle. "My father never had the sense Ola gave a goat. My mother returned here and, when he was released, he came for her.

"She gave birth to me by the side of the road." Her tone was flat. "That was the man my father was. Because of his incarceration, the Realm had seized all of their possessions, including their house, and they were forced to become Travelers."

"What's a Traveler?"

"Nomads. People who travel and fleece people for money and possessions, and they try to stay one step ahead of the Peacekeepers. We rarely stayed in one place for more than a fortnight and were constantly looking over our shoulders." She picked up a small pebble and rolled it between her thumb and forefinger. "My sister was born several years after me and things grew steadily worse. My mother became ill and lived for months on her back in a wagon as we kept moving. My father and his brother Jod were arrested again and we returned here.

"This was the first and last place I ever called home." She turned and nodded toward the stone grate and oven. "My granny taught my sister and me how to cook and bake in that fireplace. She also taught us to sew, and on cold evenings, we would sit and draw pictures and Mama would read to us." She fell silent. The weight of the past swirled around her and she could almost feel those people long gone in the room with her.

"What happened?"

"My father returned. My grandmother begged him to leave us here but he refused. He dragged us from the house." She shook her head. "My sister was little more than a baby, really. He swore no one of his blood would ever set foot here again. My mother went only because he'd taken us. She couldn't let us go without her to take care of us." Her gaze fixed on the cold stone of the fireplace. "She never saw her mother again.

"After a few moon-cycles on the road, my mother fell ill again. She spent the last year of her life confined to the wagon. She finally begged my father to rent a house in a city up north. And, for a while, it worked. He stayed out of trouble and we took care of Mama. But a few weeks after her death, we were tossed out in the streets." She shivered, feeling again the cold winter's night and the sting of the air on her skin. Never would she forget the feeling of lying in frozen mud, a Peacekeeper standing over her, so huge in his black uniform as they threw their meager possessions out into the road.

She shook the memories away. "And we went back to traveling and here I am."

"Somehow I don't think that's all the story," he said.

"Ah, you want to hear how my father sold me into slavery?" Her voice turned bitter and she saw the look of horror on his face. She flung the pebble away. "And how I was passed from man to man like some whore? Of course, not all of the men fucked me, just a few of my owners did that. One of them dressed me as a jaJin and paraded me like a pet on a leather leash. He never let his friends touch me, but they could look all the same." She waved her hand to indicate her body. "You talk about how beautiful I am, but all I see is a whore who did what she had to do to survive." She stalked past him, but he grabbed her arm. "Let go—"

He pulled her tight against him and kissed her, and at first, she resisted. She wanted nothing of tenderness from this man and she didn't deserve it. But her fists knotted in his shirt and, almost against her will, she leaned into him, her emotions raw and heart heavy.

He broke the kiss. "You survived." His breath was warm against her lips. "You survived and that's what counts. It doesn't matter what other men did to you, Nova. They don't matter and their actions don't either. Only you matter."

"You're a fool." She wanted to push him away, but her heart was beating too loudly. She wanted so much to hear and believe what he was telling her, even if she was a fool for needing it.

"I've heard that before."

He kissed her on the forehead and she melted inside, suddenly weary. "I proved him wrong."

"Who?"

"My father. He said that his blood would never enter this house again. I proved him wrong. I bought it last year just to prove him a liar."

He chuckled. "Well, you accomplished that." He propped his chin on her head and his arms tightened around her. "I think you bought it to prove he didn't break you. By selling you into slavery, he made you who you are today."

She gave a self-deprecating snort. "And what is that? A whore who learned to fleece people better than he could?"

"A woman who did what she had to do to survive in a cruel world."

She closed her eyes. "My grandmother died alone."

"And she loved you and your mother and sister. I'm sure not a day went by that you didn't think of her and she of you."

Mute, she nodded.

"There is no greater gift that can be given than to be remembered by those who loved you." He kissed her on the temple.

Nova opened her eyes. The golden rays of the sun were sinking into the ocean, setting it afire with streaks of pink and gold.

"Where is your sister?"

"Dani?" She pulled out of his arms and scrubbed her cheeks with her hands. "I don't know. Once I was sold, I never managed to track her down again. I don't know if she's dead or alive." Her heart constricted at the thought of her solemn little sister and what might have happened to her.

"Once we get the house done, we can start tracking your sister." Wyn slid his arm around her waist and led her from the house. "But first, let's inspect that package you brought back from town."

She couldn't help but laugh. "You only think of your stomach."

He gave her a lecherous wink. "And a few other body parts."

CR SO

"We found her." Ber was breathless as he raced into the room. "She's bought a house near Wryven."

"Good work." Evi shoved the prostitute off his lap. "Go down to the kitchens and gather some supplies. We'll be off in less than an hour."

Ignoring the pout on the beautiful whore's face, he strode to his desk. He needed to send a note to the countess informing her that a delivery would be forthcoming.

Chapter Eight

The moon was high overhead as they walked along the beach, their fingers entwined. The sand underfoot still held the warmth of the day. The ocean licked at Wyn's toes as they headed toward the house and the bonfire that still burned on the cliff.

"Tell me of your life in the sea." Nova's voice was quiet. He knew she was still raw from her earlier confessions and he longed to hold her and tell her it didn't matter, but he knew she wouldn't hear him. Soon she'd understand what he'd said and hopefully she'd take it to heart.

"What do you want to know?"

"I don't know anything about your kind. Where do you live? What do you eat? How do you earn money—?"

He turned and cut her flow of words by pressing his fingertip to her lips. In the glow of the moon, she looked like a goddess of old. Her hair was wild about her shoulders and she was dressed in a simple white chemise. He traced her upper lip with his finger and longed to tell her what he was thinking, but it would do no good for them now.

He let his arm drop and they continued their slow walk. "There are many clans of mer-people. Some, like me, come to the shores while others remain in the ocean all of their lives. Those clans have a tendency to live further out to sea."

"Are there any merwomen?"

"We call them mermaids. We live in houses or caves, we marry and have children, though not necessarily in that order." He raised her hand and brushed his lips across her knuckles. "Sound familiar?"

She pulled away. "Are you married?"

"No." He tugged her back. "But my parents both think it's long past time I marry."

"And why haven't you?"

"I guess I haven't found the right woman yet."

She gave a grunt of acknowledgement, her head down, her long locks hiding her face from him. They both knew he'd leave, and at that moment, it was more apparent than ever.

He pointed to the inky darkness in the south. "It's a magical place to live."

"Why haven't I heard of this place?"

"Very few humans have ever ventured there. It's only visible to the human eye within a few minutes of sunset."

"Really?"

He nodded. "As for money, we don't need much. We live off the sea and, when we need it, we make money by fishing and selling our take at the land dweller markets. Some craft jewelry from shells and others braid strong ropes of underwater vines. We aren't as different as you might think."

She shot him a disbelieving look. "I think you're very different."

"How? We love our families, we educate our children, we have a king, a form of government, industry... What's different other than the fact we have webbed hands and feet?"

She ran her thumb over the webbing between his thumb and forefinger. "What's it like down there? I mean, I love to

212

swim, but I can't go very deep. What's it like to go down so deep you think your lungs will burst?"

"It's peaceful, quiet and a world like no other. In the daylight, the water is blue-green and it's populated with beings the human eye has never seen. The pace is lazy and the wonders are endless."

"I'd like to see this place you describe." Her tone was wistful. "This place of peace."

He gave her hand a squeeze. There was no way he could take her to the depths. The pressure of the water would crush her lungs, but there was something he could share with her.

"Come on." He tugged her toward the water.

"Where are we going?"

"I can show you some of my world."

Her resistance faded as they entered the sea. He guided her into the water then up onto his back. He showed her how to lock her ankles around his waist and, once he was sure she was secure, they set off.

He headed out to sea, his body easily assuming the movements that could propel him for miles without tiring. He could feel her clutching his shoulders and her shouts of laughter rang loud as they moved through the water. He took her far out, farther than any human would ever dare to swim alone, until the bonfire was but a speck on the horizon. Overhead the moon was full and stars twinkled in the ocean as well as the sky.

Fastening her arms around his neck, he took her underwater to swim through rock formations he knew she could barely see. He showed her how to catch ticklefish and laughed when they tickled her hands with their distinctive fins. Under the light of the moon, he showed her how his people sang.

He could have stayed there forever with her.

Only they didn't have forever.

Swimming in a wide circle, he headed back as fast as he could, reveling in her shouts of delight as they cruised through the waves. When they neared the beach, she slid off his back and hand in hand they walked onto the beach.

"That was magnificent." She collapsed into a breathless heap on the sand.

No, she was magnificent.

Suddenly ravenous for her, he grabbed her shoulders. Her laughter was cut off in mid-note as their lips met. Her surprise turned to heat as their mouths devoured each other. He stroked her breasts; her nipples were hard against his palms. Without a second thought, he destroyed her chemise, rending it in two to get to her warm female flesh beneath.

She moaned as he teased her nipples and her hands stroked his chest. Her talented fingers zeroed in on his nipples as well, subjecting them to the same spine-tingling treatment. Too hungry to wait, he slid his hands up her thighs to her woman's flesh. He broke the kiss and looked down at her. On her face, he saw need and heat.

"I need you, now."

Nova nodded, her breath coming in gasps. She opened her thighs, the moon painting her flesh silver. She slid her hands around his cock and guided him into her. Thrusting forward, he buried himself in her damp heat.

Her slim legs twined his waist, her heels digging into his buttocks, urging him to move. Her hips arched and he pushed a bit more and, with a fierce growl, he began to move within her. She twisted on the sand, her cries increasing as she rushed toward her peak. Beneath him, she was the cool moon and the heat of the sun at all once. He took her deeper and faster than he could remember ever taking a woman.

Her body tensed and her muscles clenched his cock. He tried to stop his forward momentum, but it was too late. She convulsed and took him to the edge. He threw his head back and cried his completion to the sky.

Slowly he sank, her body cradling his as she murmured nonsensical words into his ear. He rested his forehead on her shoulder and wondered how he could bear to ever leave this woman.

Chapter Nine

Nova stroked the fine linen skirt of a ready-made dress. The rich emerald color did little to inspire a feeling other than mild interest. To be quite honest, she really wasn't in the mood to shop. Something didn't feel right, something she couldn't quite put her finger on.

She drifted to a table of ladies' undergarments and began sifting through a pile of lacy camisoles. The memory of Wyn tossing hers into the sea caused her to wince and she turned away from the task. Maybe she'd look at drawers.

The basket of ladies' garments was piled high and she bit her lip as she riffled through them. Silk, finely woven cotton, satin and lace... They were all tumbled together. Such was the way of the Wryven market.

She turned away from that basket as well.

Her shopping trip had been a waste of time. She didn't feel like buying anything other than the foodstuffs she'd been forced to travel for. She'd have to arrange for regular deliveries once Wyn was gone. She sighed. Even knowing that she carried enough gold coin in her pocket to buy anything she wished failed to cheer her. She moved back to the rack of ready-made clothes.

"Are you going to buy anything, girl?" She looked up at the red-faced matron of the stall. She was a large woman with three overfed horse-faced children behind her. She cast a contemptuous glance at Nova's plain clothing. "I'll see the color of your coin now before you run your grubby hands over my wares."

"Indeed." She fished the gold deuce out of her pocket and held it up so the woman could see its value. "I was going to shop here and now I've changed my mind." Ignoring the woman's spluttering, she turned away.

Seething, she stomped through the marketplace. Arranged just off the main road to Wryven, the market was a sprawling warren of nooks and crannies packed with goods. Well familiar with such places, Nova was careful to remain alert and keep her money close at hand. One of the first things her father had taught her was how to pick the pocket of the unsuspecting.

"Hey, lady, you need some pretties for your home?" a wizened woman called to her. "These were crafted by Lady Wryven herself."

"Indeed." She couldn't prevent the answering smile. "And why would Wryven's lady need to sew for a living?"

"She said her grandmother taught her." She beckoned Nova closer. "It keeps her hands busy, says she."

The stall was covered in pieces of fine linen, each stitched with silken threads. The needlework was fine, delicate and obviously the work of an accomplished needlewoman.

"These are very beautiful." She ran her hand over a table runner with an intricate ivy design on each end.

"Indeed. She's very talented." The woman pulled a tablecloth out from under a pile and held it out.

Nova froze when she saw the design. The detailed pattern of waves and shells looked almost exactly like the design on the mantel of her home. It reminded her so much of her family that her heart almost broke.

She picked up the cloth. "You said the Lady of Wryven stitched this?"

"Aye. She married Count Haaken but a few months past and she's a welcome addition to the household, if I may be so brazen to say."

"Where does she come from?" She touched the threads of a pale brown shell and the silks felt oddly warm.

"No one really knows where she came from." The woman shuffled her wares, reordering the already meticulous stacks. "Lord Haaken brought her home and married her within a fortnight." She gave a wild cackle of laughter and leaned forward, her eyes alight with merriment. "He is very handsome, is our lord. She probably couldn't wait any longer than that."

Nova smiled, though a hollowness invaded her stomach. "And her name. What is her name?"

"Her name? Her name is Lady D—" The woman broke off just as Nova felt the prick of steel slice her shirt and cut into a few layers of skin.

"Mistress Nova, how very good to see you again."

Evi's cool voice sounded in her ear and she froze. Her heart thudded as he twisted the knife ever so slightly. She felt blood run down her side. Forcing herself to remain calm, she spoke. "Hello, Evi."

He laughed and it wasn't pleasant. "I see you remember me."

She fixed her gaze on the little woman and lowered the cloth to the pile. The woman was staring at her, all merriment gone from her expression. Her eyes were dark with fear and a touch of anger.

"How could I forget you?" Nova asked. "Though I must say it's a surprise to see you here in Wryven. What can I do for you?"

"I think you know what I've come for." Evi removed the knife from her side. Taking her arm, he turned her around and reached into her blouse to retrieve her bodice knife. "I'll take that for now."

"I no longer know where Wyn is. He left several days ago." Evi had changed since the last time she'd seen him. His clothes were much shabbier than she'd remembered and his hair was mussed.

He glanced at the merchant, then back to Nova. "This is too public for our conversation." He jerked his head toward the edge of the marketplace where horses and carts were parked. "Let's just walk over this way."

Nova offered the merchant a warm smile. "Thank you for letting me see your lovely wares." She retrieved a silver coin from her pocket that would more than pay for the cloth. "I'd like this one."

The woman gave Evi a distrustful glance. "You're sure?"

"Yes, I'm sure. I'll return when I have more time to shop." She rolled up the cloth and tucked it inside her shirt and gave the woman another false smile before Evi pulled her away.

Steering her through the market, the crowds thinned as they approached the area set aside for parking. The scent of roasting meat and baked potato hash turned her stomach.

"Let's visit your home, shall we?" he said. Now that there was no one to note his actions, he didn't bother being gentle with her. He shoved her at the peddler's wagon and she hit the door with a thud.

She rubbed her abused elbow. "Wyn isn't there—"

He held up the knife and the tip was stained with her blood. "You'd better think again, woman."

She held up her hands and shook her head. "I can't tell you anything else. He left and all I know is that he lives in the sea and he's returned to it."

"Then you'll bring him back."

"I can't—"

Ber and Dreg stepped out from behind the wagon. Her breath caught when Ber grabbed her by the throat and slammed her against the door. Rage was written on every inch of his face.

"She's not being very cooperative, boss." He leered. "I think I can soften her up a bit, if you know what I mean."

All three men laughed at the crude joke and Nova refused to respond. It wouldn't be the first time she was raped and she'd already proven she could survive worse.

"Release her."

Ber relaxed his grip and she gulped for breath. Her throat felt like it was on fire from the abuse.

"Not yet. We'll take her back to her place and maybe I'll let you have her when Kelwyn returns. He can watch." Evi replaced the dagger in a hip sheath. "Put her in the wagon."

"With pleasure." Ber gave her a chilling smile as he brought down his meaty hand and she knew nothing else.

CR SO

Wyn wasn't sure how it happened. One minute he'd been varnishing the kitchen table and the next he was being held at sword point by Ber.

220

"Hello, fishy fishy," the man taunted.

The peddler's wagon lumbered up the lane with Dreg driving and Evi seated beside him. The clang of iron shackles hanging off the side turned his stomach. Silently he thanked the universe that Nova was safe in Wryven.

"Well, well, we meet again." Evi leapt down from the high seat. "I've spent a lot of time and effort to find you."

"I'm touched, though I can't say I've done the same." Wyn rose from his seat.

"Yes, well, I have more to gain from our profitable relationship than you do." Evi retrieved a pair of shackles from where they hung off the side of the wagon. "Ber, Dreg, bring me his present."

Rage welled in his chest as the men ran around the wagon. He could hear the clank of metal against metal as they opened the numerous locks that had been used to keep him inside.

If they thought he'd put on those shackles again—

Then Dreg came around the wagon with something in his arms. He walked toward Wyn and, when he was several feet away, he dumped it on the ground. Nova groaned and rolled onto her back.

Her throat was bruised and her shirt was stained with blood. Her wrists and ankles were bound with shackles that branded her as a slave.

"You bastard," he snarled.

"Now you have a choice, my friend. Either you come willingly or I sell her into slavery. She'll make a beautiful whore, won't she?" Evi tossed the shackles at him and they landed at his feet with a grotesque clang. "Men will pay a lot to fuck her." He dropped into a crouch and removed a slim dagger from a waist sheath. "She could be a little gold mine." He slashed her shirt, baring her breasts. "Not as much as you, though."

"I will destroy you," Wyn snarled.

Evi held the blade near her throat. "I don't think so. I want you to put the shackles on yourself or I kill her. I want you to remember that you gave up your freedom to save her." He sneered. "Every day of your life, when you're fucking your new mistress, at her command of course, I want you to remember what you lost."

Wyn started forward, longing to wrap his fingers around Evi's chicken throat, when the prick of Ber's sword brought him up short. He was well and truly trapped. With his gaze locked on Nova's face, he picked up the shackles. They felt cold in his hands.

For her, he would give his life.

CR 80

The moment she awoke, the terrors of the past few hours slammed into her skull. Bile burned in her throat and, as she raised her hands to her face, the clink of the iron cuffs on her wrists brought back memories of the pain, horror and degradation she'd faced as a slave. Forcing the pain away, she rolled to her side to assess her situation.

Her heart sank when she saw her house was in flames. The obscene flicker of fire licked the walls and tears stung her eyes as she watched her future being devoured.

"I see you're awake." Evi came into view, and behind him, Wyn. Shackled and held at sword point, blood ran from the corner of his mouth, but, other than that, he looked much as he had when she'd left only a few short hours ago. "You've got a choice, Nova. You can save what's left of your home or you can save him."

Her gaze swung from Wyn to the house, then back again. Evi laughed as he tossed a ring of keys in the dirt several feet away.

"I think we have our answer," he said. "Put him in the wagon."

Wyn was silent as he was paraded past her at sword-point. He stared straight ahead, and when they opened the wagon door, he stepped in without a fight. The door slammed shut and she heard the rattle of the locks.

No...

She rolled to her knees and scrambled across the ground to the keys as the wagon rolled away. Her hands were shaking so badly it took several tries before she could release the locks on her shackles. As they dropped to the ground, the roof caved in with a mighty crash and a shower of sparks.

She sat back on her heels. It was gone, all of it. Her home, her possessions, her papers of freedom and her money. It had all been in the house. She'd lost everything she'd fought so hard to create.

Her chin dropped to her chest and she longed to cry like a child. Tears stung her eyes when her gaze caught on a bit of color sticking out of her shirt. She pulled the embroidered cloth from inside her tattered blouse. Her grubby fingers left dark smudges on the white material and she clenched it in her hand.

In her life, she'd lost so much. Her family, her sister, her home, her money and she wasn't going to lose Wyn, too. He may leave her, but she couldn't live her life knowing she'd failed him. She loved him too much to let him go without a fight.

She stumbled to her feet as the fireplace caved in. Turning away from the inferno, she withdrew a slim knife from her boot. It wasn't much, but it was all she had.

As a child she'd known these woods like the back of her hand. Now, many years later, it had become unfamiliar territory. Ignoring her own safety, she ran through the thickening darkness. The wagon would have to keep to the road, but she could cut them off by traveling through the woods. She jumped over a fallen tree only to trip over a rock and fall hard on her hands and knees. Ignoring the pain, she rose and continued her blind journey.

She didn't know how long she ran, only that rain was falling. Thunder and lightning shook the ground and lit the sky for scant seconds at a time. Several times she heard the distinctive sound of a tree falling, and the scent of ozone and charred wood was thick. With every step the rain fell harder until she could barely see more than a few feet in front of her. With her lungs on fire, she finally reached the empty road. Guessing that she'd actually raced ahead of them, she ran to the south only to skid to a stop when she came upon the wreck.

The peddler's cart was on its side in a ditch. A large tree limb lay across the center and Wyn's prison was crushed.

"No!" she shrieked. Was he trapped inside? Was he dead?

Dreg lay face down in the center of the road and his neck was broken. She ran past him with barely a glance. The road was slippery and she almost fell into the ditch where the cart lay. Beneath one wheel, she saw Ber's twisted body. Trapped in the bottom of the ditch, he was already covered with a foot of runoff and was clearly dead judging from the massive gash in his throat.

"Oh my goddess, not Wyn. Please not Wyn," she sobbed. She began tearing at the limb, trying desperately to get to the wagon itself.

Without warning, someone grabbed her from behind and hauled her backward. She fell onto the road at Wyn's feet.

"What are you doing, woman?" he roared.

"Saving you," she said. She shoved her wet hair out of her face. How dare he be free and walking around when she was trying to save him? She leapt to her feet, her gaze assessing, looking for any obvious injuries. Other than a few superficial cuts, he appeared in good shape.

"I don't need to be saved," he said.

"So I noticed." She rose to her feet. "Are you okay?"

"Yes." He held the reins of the horse in his hands. "Why aren't you saving your house?"

"Because I need to save you more."

"Why?"

"Because I love you."

His expression told her he didn't believe her.

"More than your money?" he asked.

She nodded. "More than anything. I couldn't let them take you away."

"If you did, you'd have your money right now."

"What's money without love? Without family?"

He shook his head, a smile tugged at the corner of his mouth. "Isn't that what I've been trying to tell you?"

"Well, I'm a little slow—"

Wyn held out his arms and Nova rushed forward. But, just before she reached him, she caught a movement out of the corner of her eye. Evi ran toward them from the shelter of the trees. His face was covered with blood and his left arm was horribly mangled and hung useless at his side. With a cry, he threw himself at Wyn's back.

Without thinking, she whirled around Wyn, her dagger at the ready. She heard Wyn make a sound of protest and he grabbed for her hand. She felt Wyn's hand curl around hers as her dagger slid home.

The look on Evi's face was almost comical as he looked down at his chest and their joined hands on the handle of the blade. His mouth opened in a silent scream as a grotesque gurgling sound came from his throat and he slid to the ground. Grimacing, Nova allowed Wyn to pull on their joined hands as the blade slid free.

In the falling rain, three men had lost their lives in the mindless pursuit of money. She looked up into the face of the man she loved. Rather than losing, she'd saved her life.

CR SO

"Do you think I'll ever find her?"

Wyn tightened his arms around Nova. They'd bedded down in the back of the cart under the stars. The house had burned to embers and two of the four walls had caved in. They had no blankets, no food and no roof over their head, only the rickety old cart where it had all begun.

"If she's still out there, you'll find her," Wyn said. "I have it on good authority you're a very determined woman."

Nova laughed, the sound rusty. "Well, you have that right."

They fell silent, listening to the crackle of burning embers.

"Where do we go from here, Wyn?"

He heard the uncertainty in her voice. "My island. I'll introduce you to my family. Once we're married, we'll start looking for your sister."

She propped herself up on her elbow and he could feel her beautiful gaze on him. "You want to marry me?"

"Isn't that the normal progression of things?" he teased. "We get married, we make babies..."

"Babies?"

"Yes, babies."

She gulped. "How many?"

"Oh, a dozen is pretty common among my people—"

Her lips moved and no sound came out. He held back his laugh. Life with Nova would always be interesting...

About the Author

To learn more about J.C. Wilder, please visit
www.jcwilder.com. Send an email to J.C. at
mailto:wilder@jcwilder.com or join her Yahoo! group to join in
the fun with other readers as well as J.C.!
http://groups.yahoo.com/group/TheWilderSide/.

Look for these titles by
J. C. Wilder

Now Available:

Thief of Hearts

Paradox I
(Titled Paradox I in digital, titled Sacrifice in print)

Paradox III
(Titled Paradox III in digital, titled Stone Heart in print)

Sacrifice

Fly With A Dragon by Rosemary Laurey

A virgin sacrifice, a not-so ravening dragon and a happy ever after.

Selected as the virgin sacrifice to the ravening dragon, Myfanwy awaits as Arragh, the fiery Dragon of Calder Bala, approaches across the sacred grove.

But Arragh comes not to destroy. Instead he carries Myfanwy off to his domain in the far mountains, and a fate far, far better than death.

Warning, this title contains: unusual and pretty much impossible explicit sex.

Heart of the Raven by J.C. Wilder

Sold into slavery to an Overseer of the Realm, Dani is determined to win her freedom and make sure her heart is possessed by no man.

For Haaken, time is running out. A family curse already condemns him to the form of the Raven and when he can find the one woman meant for him, only then will he be free.

Too bad for both of them that this woman is determined to belong to no one...

Warning, this title contains: HOT, explicit sex.

Available now in print from Samhain Publishing.
Available now in ebook from Samhain Publishing as Paradox I.

Stone Heart

The Shattered Stone by Rosemary Laurey

Tragedy, violence and treachery and a chance encounter that leads to love and the resolution of an ancient dispute.

After her parents die of the Gray Plague, Alys flees the only home she's ever known. She sets off to find her mother's kin in the far Western Lands. On the way she meets the Monarch's envoy, Ranald ven Strad. The chance meeting leads to danger and an astounding discovery.

Warning, this title contains the following: explicit sex.

After the Rain by J.C. Wilder

Li leaves her village after her family's betrayal and seeks to create a new life for herself. She accepts a job at Graystone House as the keeper of the Evil Ones—hundreds of stone gargoyles that fill a chamber from top to bottom and rumored to be the victims of the infamous Lady of Maragorn.

Li only knows that the job fills her with dread, especially when she has to deal with one statue in particular, that of Nikolaz of Riverhaven.

Warning, this title contains the following: explicit sex.

Available in print August 2008, from Samhain Publishing.
Available now in ebook from Samhain Publishing as Paradox III

GREAT CHEAP FUN

Discover eBooks!
THE FASTEST WAY TO GET THE HOTTEST NAMES

Get your favorite authors on your favorite reader, long before they're
out in print! Ebooks from Samhain go wherever you go, and work with
whatever you carry—Palm, PDF, Mobi, and more.

Samhain
Publishing ltd

WWW.SAMHAINPUBLISHING.COM

Printed in the United States
203247BV00001B/130-1023/P